THE UNBROKEN CHAIN

OWEN D. THOMAS

DORRANCE & COMPANY • Ardmore, Pennsylvania

To my wife, Edith, for the many hours of time she has freely and willingly devoted to typing, and for the many suggestions she has contributed as to the choice of words and grammatical structure to add to its refinement, I gratefully dedicate this work.

1.

Oh God, our Help in ages past,
Our Hope for years to come,
Be Thou our Guide
While life shall last
And our Eternal Home.

AFTER THE WORDS OF THE old hymn had ended and the echoes had faded, Pastor Mitchell pronounced the benediction and dismissed the worshipers assembled for the usual Sunday morning service in the old church in Wellington City. The organist pulled out the stops of the grand old organ and the postlude began. The faithful followed the pastor and his wife down the long middle aisle of the sanctuary to the rear entrance, where each worshiper was met by the customary handshake and word of greeting. Some of them took a few brief moments to commend Rev. Mitchell for his words of wisdom from the pulpit, to which the good pastor indicated his appreciation with "Thank you! Thank you!" But it could safely be said that most of those who passed through the door had been in attendance because that was what they had done each Sunday morning for as far back as their memory carried them and even before; probably the sermon had not left an impression upon them, either good or bad. Rather, more than likely, their thoughts had been elsewhere—on their midday meal, oftimes taken with their relatives or friends; on their Sunday afternoon nap; or perhaps, in pleasant weather, on a drive in the country. The rare visitor was urged to sign the guest register located on an appropriate stand in the foyer.

As they emerged from the sanctuary, the parishioners, almost all of whom were long time acquaintances, greeted one another.

"How do you do, Harry?" Ted Jamison greeted his old friend. "How are the Nelsons today?"

1

"Oh," replied Harry Nelson, "I can't really complain. I twisted my ankle a little as I came down the courthouse steps last Monday. I limped some for a few days, but the pain is practically gone now. Elizabeth has been bothered a little with her hip. Doc Horton says it's arthritis. It comes and goes. This damp weather seems to affect it some. How have you folks been?"

"Oh, fine, fine! The twins were home from New Exeter last week—spring vacation, you know. Things were pretty lively in the house for a while, but they left on the eight o'clock train this morning, so I guess Betty and I will get back to normal again in a day or two. John and Martha visited us for a couple of days, too, with the grandchildren. We really had a house full."

"Hello, Virginia," Jeannette Johnson interrupted her long-time friend, Virginia Humes, as she headed for the outside entrance. "Guess what! Steven has been accepted as a premed student at New Exeter for the fall term. We had our doubts at first. His senior grades weren't the best, what with his recent illness and all. We are so thankful and he is glad it's all settled, too. How are your children doing in school?"

"Oh, Jenny. I want to talk to you. Would you be willing to act as chairman of the program committee for our next meeting?" It was Dorothy Langley, president of the Ladies' Auxiliary, endeavoring to recruit workers.

"Oh, I hadn't really thought about it. I am pretty busy, but I suppose . . . "

Or one might have heard Carter Wellington, the banker, conversing with his friend, William Porter, the president of the local chair factory, regarding the outlook for the furniture trade. "Will it continue its present downward trend, or can it be expected to level off?"

So went the after-church fellowship. Soon all had departed, not to meet again, for the most part, until a week later when more or less the same ritual would be repeated. The custodian, old Bill Masters, would arrive later in the week to gather the used bulletins, return the hymn books to their racks on the back of the forward pew and place valuable articles left behind in the "Lost and Found" box. Old Bill, until recently, had been a faithful worshiper in the church with his wife, but Bill was alone now and his poor health made it difficult for him to travel across town early enough for the Sunday morning service.

Such Sunday morning interchanges had been occurring between these same friends and relatives, and, in previous years, between their parents and grandparents, as they worshipped and conversed in the old but eloquent frame building. Even Rev. Mitchell, a greying, stoutish figure, had been a part of their lives for many years, having performed the baptismal rites and marriage ceremonies of many of the younger members before the very pulpit from which he spoke that morning. Likewise, his predecessors had performed the same services for many of the older folks present, as well as for their ancestors.

The late nineteenth-century building, a tribute to the important and traditional lumber industry of the city, was one of the outstanding pieces of architecture of its time and had won many a commendation for its designer. The square, low-gabled front was prefaced by four columns extending from the ground to support the roof. Its gleaming white frame, with its sleek, high steeple, was a contrast against the sky. A few wide, well-worn concrete steps led into the vestibule where the worshipers would greet their friends, remove their outer wraps and, many times during the stormy winters, brush the snow from their clothing and stomp it from their boots, or lower their umbrellas, before entering the hallowed sanctuary.

Once inside the place of worship, one was awed by the several massive stained-glass windows. Stretching to the right and the left for the full length of the long aisles, the windows were etched in images of Bible scenes which revived memories of Sunday school and Bible study as a child. The two sections of walnut pews, square and uncomfortable, even though lightly padded, extended from the rear toward the front to within a few feet of the altar rail. Beyond the rail and raised by one or two easy steps was the pulpit, with the grand old organ at the extreme left, which, incidentally had been the pride of Miss Bryant, who had contributed her talents to the church for as long as most of the members could remember.

Still beyond the pulpit, with its stiff, straight-backed chairs, was the choir loft, raised by another pair of steps. Space had been provided beyond the sanctuary for the pastor's study, choir room, and Sunday school rooms for the religious education of the young. Such was the physical structure of the building the worshipers called "our church."

The early settlers of Wellington City had organized and built their first church soon after the War of Independence, following the tenets of their Wesleyan persuasion. Generations later, after the first edifice had been destroyed by fire, the present structure was raised in a style intended to reflect the affluence of most of the parishioners. In addition to the economic progress enjoyed by the members, other changes had taken place, such as a muted religious zeal and a more formal and ritualistic style; the church, more than any other in the town, gradually became the one where the elite and important figures in business and politics and, of course, the more financially successful, were to be found. Newcomers to Wellington City soon became aware that the Methodist church was the one to attend if business and financial importance played a prominent role in their lives. Also, a woman who wanted to climb the social ladder found that her acceptance into the church's ladies' group, a sometimes difficult step, was a definite asset.

Wellington City, formerly known as Union Corners, was renamed for one of its prominent early families. Anglo-Saxon adventurers, pushing westward from the Atlantic coastal plains, defying the barrier of the Alleghenies, had settled just beyond the mountains, in the gently rolling country where forests furnished a bountiful supply of lumber. A river which flowed through the area furnished an ample supply of water. On open, less hilly ground, agriculture and dairy farming became profitable.

As industry grew, so did Wellington City. Soon the town attracted those who sought steady, well-paid employment in the lumber mills, farms, dairies, and the supporting trades. It didn't require much time for easterners to realize that where there was work, with paychecks to be spent, there was also a need for merchants in clothing, food, and many other types of commodities which must be available from a local source of supply. Therefore, buildings of many types needed to be constructed, as well as businesses operated. Also, schools, churches, and other public buildings would be required, with the result that Wellington City would become more than a dot on the map.

But a city cannot grow without an adequate means of moving its products. Of course, there was the horse and wagon, but this was a slow method to use in the distribution of the products of a thriving city. When two of the country's newly formed railroads extended their tracks into Wellington City, faraway points were able to benefit from its products, further enhancing the city's trade. In addition, people, as well as cargo, were provided with a more convenient method of transportation to other cities. All in all, the railroads were a definite asset to the new city.

In time, Wellington City was to be considered of such importance that it was selected as the county seat; this necessitated the building of a courthouse, which was the subject of much controversy. Where would the new building be located? How large would it need to be to meet future needs? What type of building would be not only the most practical, but the most esthetic? What would it cost the taxpayers? The issue was the most talked-about among those whose responsibility it was to decide such things—the mayor, the county board, the county engineer, and other duly elected officials. One could also hear the subject discussed among those who had their own opinions but who had no real power to influence the local officials.

Many of Wellington City's citizens objected strenuously to the construction of the new courthouse on the site of the city's only recreational park located in a square in the center of the business area. Finally, however, "City Hall" prevailed and the building was erected in the most practical and most accessible spot—the city park site—with the assurance that a new park would be provided elsewhere. Whether or not a new park would be forthcoming would remain to be seen. But new courthouses are important, too.

As was the custom in that era, the courthouse was a "four-square" structure of concrete, two stories high, with recessed windows, double doors opening on all sides, each accessible only after climbing several steps. In the tower was a clock, with one of its four faces visible from each side of the tower, announcing the passing of the hours and of the half-hours. Once inside, the visitor was confronted by entrances to several offices from which the business of the county was conducted. On the second floor, reached by a massive open stairway, was the courtroom, with its adjacent judge's chambers, jury room, and law library. All this was set in an area surrounded by a well-kept lawn, with benches placed at strategic spots among the remaining trees, resembling in some respects the park that had been lost. Provisions for parking vehicles at the curbs of each of the four streets surrounding the site had not been overlooked.

With its railroads, industry, and various businesses, Wellington City had become the largest commercial trading center within a radius of twenty-five or thirty miles. Each passenger train would bring visitors for business or pleasure to the city, increasing the pedestrian traffic on its sidewalks.

In the growing city there was soon evidence of the development of social classes. The first, or the highest, from an economic standpoint, was comprised of the factory owners, the builders, the financiers and their heirs. This group, with their families, formed the power structure and was considered to be the elite, or the first families of the city.

Then came what is commonly called the middle class group—the small business owners of the grocery, hardware, and other shops supplying the everyday needs of the population. Most individuals of this group, just as the name implies, attained a comfortable, but not affluent, living standard. Influential politically and economically, on occasion a member of this group would manage to crash the barrier and become a member of the elite society; others, the victims of unfortunate business reverses, would find themselves left behind socially and economically, to be counted as members of the lower class.

The group designated as the lower class—manual workers, daily and hourly wage earners, and to a large extent, farmers—was also present in great numbers as in any town the size of Wellington City. Some of the larger farm owners and operators were fortunate enough, through good business acumen, to break through to a higher economic level, proving that the feudal system did not apply in America, at least not to the extent found in many places in other parts of the globe.

Then there was the professional group—physicians, dentists, lawyers, teachers, clergymen—who could be classified as members of any one of these socioeconomic groups according to whether or not the individual was financially and professionally successful in his field.

The river on which Wellington City was located provided a

power source and pond for many of the lumber mills; it also determined the residential areas for the city's inhabitants, whose living quarters were built in areas consistent with their economic status. Small frame houses on the lowlands near the river – many little more than shanties – were the homes of wage earners, manual workers, the lower class. Often, high water levels, resulting from spring thaws in the mountains combined with spring rains, would force the inhabitants of these homes to flee to higher ground for their safety, until the threat was alleviated.

The homes of the middle class were built farther from the river on higher ground. These homes, while not ostentatious, were generally comfortable and well-cared for, indicating a pride of possession. The upper class, or elite, occupied spacious homes on the bluffs, high above the river. These homes, characteristic of the era, were classified as mansions and were elaborately adorned, built at great cost; they would be considered by later generations to be impractical and lacking in style. Yet many were considered to be landmarks for their magnificent and unique architecture.

While some brick and stone were employed in the more elaborate homes as an indication of affluence, most houses, whether those of the lower, middle, or upper class, were constructed with wood, because of its plentifulness. In fact, the use of wood was so practical that even some of the city's streets were paved with blocks hewn from wood to resemble bricks, which endured well into the twentieth century.

Wellington City grew and prospered during most of the nineteenth century, but change was coming. Since decline is insidious, it is difficult to pinpoint when it first began. Toward the middle of the century, great changes were taking place. First Ohio, then the middle western states, and finally, the Great Plains were settled and rapidly became the breadbasket of America. Gold was discovered in California in 1849, and throngs of the population with their Conestoga wagons emigrated westward in search of fortune. The slavery issue in the newly formed states and the Civil War further dislocated and scattered thousands of families. Finally, the railroads spanned the breadth of the Nation and ever-increasing hordes pushed westward. Wellington City was no longer a part of the West but the East. The center of population had long ago passed her by.

As the country found itself in the rapidly developing industrial, commercial, and agricultural economy of the twentieth century, Wellington City's seemingly inexhaustible supply of lumber began to dwindle. Her factories, too, were becoming antiquated compared to the new modern complexes being constructed in the developing areas farther to the west, south, and even into what was known at the time as the "far west." The small patches of farmland in the clearings of the Allegheny foothills proved to be poor competition for the more tillable lands of the middle and far west.

Wellington City staggered, her population growth ceased. Slow but gradual decline had begun. With the passing decades, a world war, and a devastating depression which was followed by a second world war, she had lost a third of her population; work opportunities had diminished and the city, once a boom town, experienced stagnation.

Despite this series of events, the remaining population had settled more firmly than ever before into its three-class society. The elite, with its inherited wealth of bygone days, seemed even more secure and with the emigration of large numbers of the middle and lower classes in search of better opportunities, the local aristocrats consolidated their control even more securely over the economic and political life of the city. These were the parishioners who have been described at the worship service in the Wellington City Methodist Church.

2.

As WAS HIS CUSTOM, Carter Wellington closed the door of his office at the Wellington City National Bank at almost exactly noon. No need to lock the door, as he could be assured that his trusted employees would not invade the privacy of his business affairs without permission. J. Carter, as he was known among his peers, looked ahead to the six-block walk to his home to take the midday meal with his widowed mother, Martha.

The home, a large two-and-one-half-story structure, had been the dwelling of many generations of the Wellington family. Situated on a large tract of land sloping gently toward the new concrete sidewalk, the home was noted for its architecture and was one of Wellington City's most elegant. The large veranda gracing its front followed the general pattern of the turreted design. A steep gable above the veranda allowed space for the second and a half-story above. A half-circle stained-glass window permitted diffused, tinted light to enter the upstairs hallway. If the exterior of the home was elegant, the interior was no less so, with its tiled front foyer, wide circular stairway, arched doorways, a large fireplace and countless other graceful, eye-appealing splendors.

The Wellingtons were never too proud to be humble. As J. Carter approached his home he greeted Mr. Smithson who was trimming the hedge at the entrance gate.

"Hello, Bill! A neat job you are doing there. The warm weather and rain have really brought the shrubs out rapidly this year. Right?"

"Right!" replied Bill. "Those lilacs will be full out in a matter of days. The tulips were unusually beautiful this year, but they're almost gone already. Those red emperors were especially lovely.

Such gorgeous red blooms! Right away now, I want to plant petunias, geraniums, impatiens, and perhaps some snapdragons. Those will be in bloom until the frost catches 'em. That fertilizer we used on the lawn last fall sure has done the grass a world of good. We ought to give it another treatment about September. All that snow last winter gave it moisture and protection from the cold."

William Smithson had been the Wellington's faithful gardener for as long as J. Carter could remember. It was his expertise that had produced the beautiful lawn and garden, with its profusion of blossoms from April until October, that the Wellingtons, as well as passersby, enjoyed each day. The evergreens surrounding the veranda and at each side of the lot lent winter beauty not easy to describe.

Mrs. Martha Wellington, a slightly built woman of some sixty years, was waiting on the front steps enjoying the sunshine and smiling approvingly. Reserved and gracious, she looked forward to the noonday meal with her only child as much as he did.

"Right on time as usual," she greeted him.

"Of course. Coming home to lunch with my favorite girl friend is one of the highlights of my day."

She smiled more fully and exclaimed, "Carter, you always say that."

"But it's the truth, Mother, and today is such a pleasant day. The walk has been an unusual pleasure."

"Yes, I will agree with you. The sunshine here on the steps feels so good," she added. "I noticed Bill is trimming the hedge already. How did everything go at the bank this morning?" It was her usual question.

"Fine, just fine." Then as an afterthought he added, "New deposits continue to decline a little, but on the whole, deposits, reserves, and borrowings remain relatively constant despite the economic condition of the town generally—not as high as in the peak years, but yet there has been no widespread decline. The receipts and withdrawals have suffered only slightly. Part of this is attributable to former residents who still maintain their accounts with us. Apparently they must hope to return when business conditions permit, when they retire, or when their work is ended elsewhere. Since Father died, the total banking activities have declined less than ten percent. Not bad, is it, considering everything?"

"I'm glad, not only for myself and the town, but especially for you, Carter, that things have held up so well. Those who felt that you were too young to manage the bank were certainly mistaken," Martha remarked. She continued, "Even during the Depression, when Father was not in the bank, Wellington City National remained solvent and stable, being closed only by President Roosevelt's decree closing all the banks. And our bank reopened as usual the very day the banks were permitted to do so."

Carter added, "What really helped us then was the closing of the Merchants' State Bank. It was not so fortunate as we were, but we were able to take over their assets and consolidate their business into our own. That was a stroke of good luck, both for us and their depositors, since they did not have to go through the inconvenience of a long and costly liquidation to receive their money. This helped us by increasing our total volume of business at almost no extra operating cost, besides eliminating our only competition. Yes, we were indeed fortunate and this has been a contributing factor even now to our continued good fortune in resisting the decline being experienced by nearly every other business in town."

Martha nodded her agreement. She and Carter had talked about the bank's apparently solid position many times, but reiterating the story gave them reassurance.

After Carter and Martha made small talk about various subjects—layoffs as a result of the declining business conditions, household matters—during a light lunch tastily prepared by Martha, he bid her good-bye with a light kiss on the cheek and, amid her laments at his having to hurry away so soon, departed.

As Martha Wellington stood in the doorway watching her son walk down the street and slowly disappear in the distance, she admired his dignified, erect posture and the courteous, correct, and friendly manner in which he greeted passersby on the sidewalk. Her memory wandered back to his boyhood days and even beyond to her courtship with his father. Christened Martha Carter, she was born into one of the wealthy families of

Wellington City whose forebears had made their fortune in lumber. She had known James Wellington practically all her life, having attended elementary, then later high school, with him; together they had marched off to New Exeter College some forty miles distant.

New Exeter was then and continued to be the small denominational liberal arts college affiliated with the Methodist church organization and supported in part by the local church. Traditionally it attracted nearly all the college-bound youth from the Wellington City Methodist Church, as it had their parents and even their grandparents.

James Wellington had operated the bank, following the footsteps of four generations of his ancestors. It was little wonder that the fledgling community had early been renamed Wellington City after its inauspicious beginning as Union Corners. The Wellingtons, one of the pioneer families, had early entered the banking business, establishing the town's first and, for many years, its only bank. The bank had helped finance the growth of many of the early enterprises in the vigorous young community with the aid of large borrowings from older financial institutions in the East such as Harrisburg and Philadelphia—as well as from Pittsburgh, which at that time was a new but growing metropolis. Due to the sturdy conservative guiding of former generations of the Wellington family, the bank had acquired a position of independence and stability so that outside borrowings for its needs had long since become unnecessary.

When James Wellington's father had retired and handed over the management of the bank to his son, it was the citadel of wealth in Wellington City. But the son did not come ill-prepared for this responsibility. After graduating from New Exeter, he had returned to Wellington City and immediately assumed the duties of assistant and understudy to his father. Step by step, he had thoroughly learned every phase of the business. For nearly twenty years he had labored side by side with his father. When the senior Wellington became aware of fatigue due to advancing years, it was with a feeling of absolute confidence that he relinquished his responsibilities and his titles to his well-trained successor. Change in the bank's management had not come too soon, for within a few months the father was taken in death, as if he felt the time had come to hand the reins to another.

James Wellington, upon returning from New Exeter and assuming his work with his father, became betrothed to his childhood sweetheart, Martha. Since the Wellingtons and the Carters were pioneers of the community, both families had reached the level of the socially elite in Wellington City and had attended the Wellington City Methodist Church for many generations. The elder Wellingtons and Carters gave their hearty approval to the marriage, which had been one of the social events of prominence in the city.

A pompous wedding at the church took place, followed by an equally pompous reception at the local hotel. The following year, a son was born to the couple; christened James Carter Wellington, his name united the Christian name of the father and the surnames of both the families. As a child, the boy was called Carter to avoid confusion with his father. As an adult, the initial J. was annexed to indicate the existence of his father's first name. For a time he used the full name, James Carter Wellington, but economy of time and effort finally firmly established "J. Carter Wellington" as official; it was the name he preferred to use.

The boyhood history of J. Carter very much resembled that of his father. As his father had, he attended the local elementary and high schools of Wellington City, then continued on to New Exeter College. After graduating, he returned home and assumed the position as assistant and understudy to the president of the bank, his father, as tradition dictated.

But fortune was not to permit J. Carter the long apprenticeship in the business enjoyed by his predecessor. Scarcely two years after taking on his duties at the bank, misfortune struck the Wellington family. After having spent that fateful day at the bank, James Wellington returned home, read the evening newspaper, dined with his wife and son, and then joined them briefly in the family room. Shortly thereafter, he remarked to Martha, "I believe I will go to the bedroom and lie down."

Martha, somewhat alarmed because her husband usually

retired rather late, replied, "What is wrong, James? Don't you feel well?"

"It's really nothing serious. I seem to be having an uncomfortable feeling in my chest. I may be coming down with a cold, but with a little rest I am sure I will be all right. I'll take an aspirin." Whereupon he retired to his room.

Martha was especially apprehensive. Her husband had always been a healthy man and she could not remember the last time he had complained of being ill. Some thirty minutes later she quietly opened the door to the room to check on him. The regular, familiar sounds of his breathing led her to believe that all was well, and she returned to the family room relieved. Later, she went to the bedroom to join her husband in retiring. Carter, who was still in the family room, heard a shout. "Carter, come here! Something is wrong with Dad!"

Rushing into the bedroom at his mother's command, Carter found his father without pulse or heartbeat. All efforts to arouse him or to discover some vital life signs proved futile. With the arrival of the family physician, it was revealed that James Wellington had suffered a massive coronary occlusion and that death had been almost instantaneous. After Rev. Mitchell conducted the funeral at the Methodist church, which had played so prominent a role in the family's social and religious life, James Wellington was laid to rest in the adjoining cemetery alongside his ancestors.

At the time of his father's death, J. Carter was only in his mid-twenties and had had scarcely two years of training in banking. There were murmurings that the presidency of the bank should pass to an older, more experienced employee. But Martha Wellington had different ideas. By reason of her late husband's bequest, she was the owner of nearly all of the outstanding stock in the bank. She was adamant that the family chain of command remain unbroken and that her son, J. Carter, succeed to all the titles, functions, and powers exercised by his father, notwithstanding his short period of apprenticeship and relative youth. Who could dispute her? She possessed the votes. Thus it was that young J. Carter Wellington became president and chairman of the board of directors of the Wellington City National Bank.

Fourteen years had passed and J. Carter had skillfully managed the bank with the characteristic conservatism of his predecessors. At the same time, he had broken the monotony of what would otherwise have been a lonely widowhood for his mother by assuming his father's role as the head of the household, acting as a constant companion for his mother and as escort to those social functions which she cared to attend. So close were mother and son that J. Carter had dismissed the idea of marriage and separation from his mother completely from his mind. If J. Carter ever thought of life without his mother, he never gave voice to such thought. It seems that he believed he would always have her, that she would be immortal.

3.

THE PORTERS WERE ANOTHER of the earliest pioneer families to settle in what was then Union Corners. First entering into the lumber trade, the Porters later became manufacturers of chairs of such quality that the demand for their product created the necessity for a large factory, thus adding substantially to the growth of the town later known as Wellington City. Following the usual pattern, financing was obtained, in part, from the local bank operated by another early family, the Wellingtons.

Because of good management practices and sales expertise, the enterprise prospered and the loans were liquidated in quick order. Within two generations the Porters became one of Wellington City's most important and wealthiest families along with the Carters and Wellingtons; of course, they too had joined the elite of the Wellington City Methodist Church.

During the early years of the twentieth century, under the management of John Porter II, the Porter Chair Company had reached the pinnacle of its production. Then, for reasons not quite understood by those whose lives it affected, a slow decline began to take place. What was happening? Was Wellington City's principal industry and the foundation of its success crumbling?

"What do you gentlemen think?" John Porter II was asking his board of directors at the regular monthly meeting. "We can give up, or we can attack the problem by backing away and giving it a good hard look from a new and different perspective. Perhaps the answer is to call in some outside consultants to analyze our problems. Perhaps we even need new blood."

After considerable discussion, Frank Swift, a longtime member, moved that the company make whatever changes

16

might be necessary to stay in competition with newer plants farther west, using its excellent credit references and reputation to obtain any necessary financing. The motion was seconded by James Kennedy, another faithful board member. The measure passed by a unanimous vote.

At this time, John Porter II retired and passed the management to his eldest son, William. John felt that after twenty-five years as president of the company, a younger, more vigorous man could generate some new ideas, giving the business "a shot in the arm," so to speak.

Under the able management of William Porter, modern machinery was installed and new and more efficient methods were initiated; the business prospered, not to the extent that it once had, but vigorously enough that the company could compete with the more modern plants without, happily, incurring debts. The Porter wealth continued to grow, and the family was able to maintain its coveted place in the business and social circles of Wellington City.

As a young man, William Porter had married Sarah Owens, the daughter of another of Wellington City's pioneer families who had engaged in and earned a fortune in the building and construction industry. The Owens family, too, due to their success, were members of the same social group as the Wellingtons, Carters, and Porters, making them intimate friends through many generations and influential members of the Wellington City Methodist Church.

Sarah and William Porter's two children brought them much happiness. William, Jr., interesting and intelligent, was an outstanding student and in his parents' mind would one day succeed his father as the president of the Porter Chair Company. Jane, two years younger, was poised, graceful, and an altogether proper youngster, excelling equally with her brother in scholastic aptitude. But, alas, the Porters were to be left with only their daughter. A swimming accident occurred while the family was on vacation at the seaside the summer young Bill was fourteen.

Grief-stricken, the family returned home, and in the years to follow the parents appreciated their daughter even more than before. After high school, she was sent to New Exeter, and since

17

it would hardly be possible for her, a woman, to be acceptable as the head of her father's business, she elected to major in literature and language, graduating four years later magna cum laude.

Returning home after graduation, Jane wrestled with her future. She was well-prepared for any one of a number of fields. One evening during the dinner hour, the subject of which field she would pursue was being discussed.

"Father," Jane said, "what is wrong with me taking a position in the company as a secretary?"

"Nothing really, but the feeling today is that a woman could never hope to advance to a managerial position, and being a mere secretary the rest of your life is hardly an ambition for a girl from your station in life."

Jane reasoned, "But, Father, that would be just for a starter, just to get the feel of being useful, of getting acquainted with the business world."

"But, Jane, you know you are not only welcome to remain here in our home, we would enjoy having you," interjected Sarah. "You and I could have some enjoyable hours here. You have been away most of the time for four years. I would like to get acquainted with you again."

"Mother, I have never been able to experience the work-a-day world. I need that experience."

"Well," Jane's father commented, "we'll see where there might be an opportunity for you to really use your talents. Have you ever considered teaching, or writing? Writing, particularly, can be a noble profession, a very valuable service. Classroom teaching can never hope to rival writing for those who are really talented."

"That does arouse my interest."

After some weeks had passed, during which Jane enjoyed being at home with her mother, there appeared in the mailbox a letter addressed to Jane from New Exeter College.

"What can this be about?" she remarked to her mother.

"I wonder. Probably soliciting funds for a new library or a new dormitory. All the present buildings are old and need replacing or enlarging, and other buildings should be added."

Slitting open the letter, Jane read:

Dear Miss Porter,

New Exeter College is indeed happy to add your name to our list of distinguished literary graduates. As you know, we are currently in the process of upgrading our library. We need top-notch people on our staff. Would you possibly be interested in helping us?

Let me assure you that while the salary will not be great, the work would be rewarding.

May we hear from you soon?

The letter was signed by Dr. Harry S. Stanford, President.

"What do you think, Mother?" said Jane as she finished reading the letter. "Library work is interesting. As you know, I have had some experience along that line by working one day a week in the library while I was in school. I would have enjoyed working there more frequently, but I did not feel I had the time. In fact, I had entertained ideas of majoring in library science. Well, I shall think it over. I'll see what Father thinks."

Jane read the letter again. "It was very thoughtful of Dr. Stanford to consider me," she thought as she carried the communication to her room to give the offer some serious thought in private.

That evening at dinner Jane told her father about the letter and the offer.

"I think that would be great. But you are an adult now, almost twenty-three, and college-trained. It is your decision."

The following day Jane posted a letter to Dr. Stanford, requesting an interview. Two days later she received a telephone call and an interview was arranged for early the next week.

It was with high expectations that Jane entered Dr. Stanford's well-appointed office. After some preliminary inquiries about her family and other small talk, her interviewer came to the point.

"Well, Miss Porter, what do you think about working in our library? Your major was literature, which would serve you well for that type of work. I see by your records that you served one day a week in the library while you were in school. I might add, too, that Mrs. Johnson, the head librarian, will be retiring at the end of this year, and you would be in line for her position."

"Yes, I did serve in the library part-time, and I enjoyed the work very much. I believe I would be happy working full-time in that field. You would want me to start at the opening of the fall semester, I suppose."

"Before we talk about that, let's talk about salary. You probably realize the college at this time is barely solvent and does not have a wide margin of finances. What would you expect in the way of salary?"

Jane responded that salary was not really important. "It is the idea of being useful and contributing something to humanity, of stimulating people to read good literature, that intrigues me," she said.

"Would you be willing to accept the equivalent of the salary we are paying Mrs. Johnson?"

Jane was agreeable.

"Very well. We'll plan on you beginning work at the beginning of the fall semester?"

"That will be fine," Jane agreed excitedly.

In September, after an interesting summer with her parents, part of which had been spent at the family's vacation spot, Jane assumed her duties as assistant librarian at New Exeter. At the end of December, Mrs. Johnson ended her longtime service and Jane was elevated to the position of head librarian. Her fondness for the work compensated for the small salary she received.

Although living on the campus, Jane returned home at intervals of a few weeks. During her weekend visits home she shared with her parents her pleasure at meeting again her old friends both in the student body and on the faculty at the college, as well as the new friends she had acquired. After nearly seven years of enjoyable and rewarding work, she observed on one of her regular visits home that her mother was not the active, animated woman she had been, and her features appeared haggard and drawn. Upon questioning, Sarah admitted she had lost some weight and was not feeling quite up to her old self.

Apprehensively, Jane returned to New Exeter, not neglecting her weekly letters it had been her custom to write. One evening she received a telephone message. Her father was calling to express his concern for Sarah's health. She had visited her physician that day and had been admitted to the hospital for observation. Jane secured a brief leave of absence to be with her parents, to show her concern.

Tests at the hospital revealed that Sarah was suffering from what could be a dread disease which was very often fatal. Dr. Franklin, their longtime physician, spoke with William and Jane. "I am sorry, but I must report that the tests show that Mrs. Porter may have an intestinal tumor. With your authorization, I will call in Dr. Hinson, from Erie, a specialist in abdominal surgery, for a consultation. He will order a further examination to determine if such is the case and to ascertain whether or not surgery would be beneficial."

After Dr. Hinson's examination, the consultation took place between the two physicians and it was determined that surgery would be necessary to discover the exact extent of the tumor and verify its probable malignant nature.

After the surgery, it was Dr. Franklin's sad duty to report to William and Jane that Dr. Hinson had advised him that a malignancy did, in fact, exist and was already widespread, having extended to vital organs which could not be removed.

Sarah was able to return to her home after some days, her true condition unknown to her. Reluctantly but dutifully, Jane arranged an extended leave of absence from her position at the college to be at home with her distraught father and to be a companion to her mother. Even though Sarah had not been apprised of the seriousness of her condition, Jane's continued absence from the college library made her suspicious.

"Jane, aren't you going to return to New Exeter?" Sarah asked her daughter after several days at home.

"Oh, mother, I have had a very steady routine for several years. I have decided I would like to be at home for a while, especially until you get to feeling better. I can always go back when I am ready."

Sarah accepted Jane's explanation, but she felt a gnawing uneasiness. It was not for long, therefore, that Jane and William could hide from Sarah the true extent of her illness. She could no longer be convinced that she would recover. The best day and night special-duty nurses were employed to attend Sarah and to make her as comfortable as possible, but death won before many months had passed. Jane and William Porter were alone.

William did not ask Jane to resign her position at the college, but Jane declared, "Father, I could never leave you alone here to brood over our loss. I feel that Mother would have wanted me to make a home for you as she has done for so many years. The day has not come when a daughter would be expected to assume the management of a large business—that, as yet, is considered to be a man's field—but she is expected, if the need arises, to be a homemaker and companion to her father, the only father she will ever have. And that is what I intend to do."

"But Jane, I can't ask you to do that. You have your own life to live, and I want you to be happy. I'll get along. I'll wrap myself up in the business. Other men have faced the same situation. Don't you remember Mr. Jackson, the publisher? He has been alone many years."

"Yes, I admire the man for facing life realistically, but he is in a different position. His sons and daughters are all living at a distance and have their own families."

"Very well, if that is what you want to do. But I am not going to insist that you do it."

That very day Jane dispatched her letter of resignation to New Exeter College. Dr. Stanford, with mixed emotions, replied quickly.

Dear Miss Porter:

It was with deep regret that I read of your mother's death. It is also with deep regret that I cannot do otherwise than accept your resignation. I must commend you, however, for your noble decision. Life sometimes presents us with difficult choices.

I speak on behalf of the entire staff when I express how much your contribution to the college has been appreciated. If ever your situation changes and you wish to return to the college in any capacity, please do not hesitate to let us know.

Sincerely,

Dr. Harry Stanford, President

Five years had passed since Jane made that important decision which she had never regretted. She had filled her place well as a companion and homemaker for a grateful father and had resumed the activities of the religious and social group she had left behind in Wellington City eleven years before upon entering New Exeter—first as a student and later as a member of the staff.

4.

*T*HE FOLLOWING WINTER Wellington City experienced one of its periodic outbreaks of influenza, or what was more commonly called by the older residents "grippe." Not everyone was affected, but many of the city's residents experienced the temporarily debilitating effects of the disease. After a few days of enforced bedrest, nearly all the victims slowly recovered and returned to their normal activities.

As friends met on the street, in their homes, or in the grocery stores and other places, one would hear such conversations as "Hello, Betty. How are you?"

"Oh, I'm fine now, but the family, including me, was laid up with the grippe for a few days, but we are all feeling better now."

"Oh, is that right?" answered her friend, Hazel Browning. "We all had it, too, about three weeks ago. Grandpa Bert, especially. It only lasted a day or two for most of us, but the old gentleman still hasn't completely recovered."

"How is Grandpa now?"

"Well, he is doing better, but you know Grandpa is nearly eighty now and with his heart condition, he doesn't spring back as fast as the rest of us."

"I guess it does affect the older folks a little more. I think, though, by now almost everyone has weathered the worst of it and, fortunately, on the whole, it has been rather mild, except for a few cases."

"That's true, but for a day or so it can really knock you out."

"You said it! For a couple of days it can really lay a person so low that he doesn't care if he lives or dies."

Alice Johnson joined in, "So far our family has escaped it, but I hear some folks are still having quite a time of it."

At the J. Carter Wellington household, the disease followed the course of one of the "few cases." Martha Wellington, never a

24

robust woman, had gradually become even more frail during her fifteen years of widowhood. Now in her early sixties, she was showing the ravages of age more rapidly than most women, especially in view of the advantaged life to which she was accustomed. Especially prone to respiratory diseases, when Martha fell victim to the "flu," the disease did not treat her lightly.

When her temperature had remained high for several days, Dr. Franklin suggested Martha be taken to the hospital where her illness was diagnosed as pneumonia. Despite the administration of all known medication and treatment, her body could not overcome the ravages of the disease and death came within a few days.

As he had for many of his congregation throughout the years, Pastor Mitchell performed the funeral rites and Martha was laid to rest beside her husband in the Wellington family plot in the church cemetery.

With the responsibility of arranging the funeral and acknowledging the condolences of his social, church, and business acquaintances as well as those of many of the towns-folk who had met him at the bank, Carter had not had an opportunity to dwell upon the future. The evening of the day of the funeral, William Porter had kindly invited him to have dinner with him and Jane, which he gladly accepted. William and Jane deliberately directed the conversation from the events of the last few days to other subjects, such as national events and local activities. William thought back to a few years earlier when he was faced with a similar situation and how much he had appreciated the thoughtfulness of friends. But he still had Jane. Carter was alone.

Carter seemed to listen and even joined in the conversation, but there was that sense of irreplaceable loss within himself. "Must I go now to a house – it's not a home now – where there is no one waiting for me at the front gate?" he thought to himself. "Yes, I must. There will be Ellen, the housekeeper, and Mr. Smithson will be around tomorrow. I'll just have to carry on." With those thoughts Carter returned to the only home he had ever known and to reality.

The next morning, Ellen, the dedicated housekeeper, prepared the usual breakfast of eggs, bacon, toast, coffee, and juice which she had prepared for years for Martha and Carter, but Carter barely touched the food.

"Now, Mr. Wellington, you must take some nourishment." But even Ellen didn't feel like eating. She had become one of the household and with Mrs. Wellington absent, it just wasn't the same.

Before Carter left the table, Bill entered the room and greeted him. Even though there wasn't much yard work during the winter, Bill would come daily to the Wellington house — after all, there was often snow to remove from the walks and things to be fixed around the house. Even he felt the emptiness of the house. At a loss for words to fit the circumstances, Bill asked, "Shall I wash the windows today? It's the first sunny day we've had for a while and it's not too cold."

Carter, even though not really wanting to think of such things, replied, "Yes, busy yourself with anything you choose."

Carter then went into his own room to think awhile. He tried to read and listen to the radio, but he couldn't put his mind to anything. He stared out the window. He lay on the bed.

Finally, in the late afternoon, he decided to go to the office in an effort to occupy himself. As he entered the building, Mr. James, his assistant was just leaving — the business day was over.

"Oh, I didn't expect you in today!"

"I didn't expect to be here either," Carter replied, "but I thought I might as well try to get my mind off myself." After an hour or two of trying to peruse some documents that had been placed on his desk during the last few days, Carter returned to the four walls of the big house.

During the next few days the big old house became even more unbearable to Carter. He spent a few hours each day at his office. In the evening, he would seek his old friends and delay his return home to a late hour. Sunday came and before the morning service William Porter once again graciously invited Carter to join him and Jane for dinner, which he accepted with thanks.

During the meal the conversation was again carefully directed away from Carter's bereavement. Carter deliberately encouraged Jane to relate some of her experiences during the last few years since leaving New Exeter. Even though Jane was making a home for her father, it did not mean that she had no time for activities outside the home. William had encouraged her to pursue useful and enjoyable interests about the town. One of these interests was volunteer work at the local library. In this manner she was able to keep abreast of the latest books, some of which Carter, an avid reader, had already read. They discussed these and discovered that their literary tastes were much the same.

The conversation continued throughout the afternoon and evening. Recognizing the many common interests between Carter and Jane, William had little to say, except to indicate his attentiveness to the conversation by occasionally making an appropriate remark. Not wishing to exclude the older man from their conversation, Carter would sometimes seek William's opinion on certain issues of the day. But for the most part, it was Jane and Carter who did not allow the conversation to lag.

Finally, Carter declared, "As much as I dislike the idea, it is time for me to go. William, you no doubt will want to be at the office early tomorrow. I can't tell you how much I have appreciated being with you folks today. It would have been a long, lonely day had it not been for you."

"Let me assure you," Jane replied, "the pleasure has been ours as much as yours. We have each lived in this town all our lives; we were born here, grew up here, and have known each other ever since we can remember. Yet it seems that this afternoon we have really become acquainted. Why is it that it takes a tragedy or a disaster to bring people together?"

"It does seem a shame, doesn't it?" observed Carter, looking at the floor to hide the sadness that came over his face at the mention of his tragedy.

"Would you like to accompany Father and me to the Wednesday Evening Family Night at the church?" Carter and Martha had been regulars at the fun and worship event each week until her illness, and she and Carter had been in attendance there only three weeks before.

Carter hesitated. "Do you think it would be proper?"

"I don't see why not. You wouldn't need to participate in the games or the program. It would at least occupy your time and bring you into the company of others."

27

William agreed with Jane, and Carter, with mixed emotions, accepted.

After taking leave of the Porters, the loneliness again overwhelmed Carter, but what else could he do at that late hour but return home and take a sedative which Dr. Franklin had prescribed, and go to bed?

Carter awoke the next morning feeling in somewhat better spirits. He was thinking about Jane and the pleasant afternoon he had experienced the day before in her home. He had known Jane casually for many years, but it had not been until yesterday that he had been aware of her extraordinary qualities. "Am I falling in love with her?" he mused to himself. He couldn't be sure, but he liked the idea. Or was he just merely lonely for companionship?

Aside from the telephone calls from the Porter home, one from William and the other from Jane, on Monday and Tuesday evenings, Carter had no contact with the Porters until Wednesday evening. Although feeling somewhat sad that Martha was missing from the group at the Family Night activities, Carter appreciated being with the Porters, especially Jane. The other members present extended their warm greetings and expressed their happiness that he had come.

Jane and her father had always been agreeable companions but the quarter-century difference in age could not be ignored. His thoughts, his views, were not necessarily Jane's thoughts nor her views. William neither requested nor expected that Jane would not seek company of her own age in her social group. Carter's needs were the same as Jane's and he sought the fulfillment of those needs in the same group. Consequently and inevitably, they would be seeing a lot of each other. Only a relatively few years separated their ages. Their backgrounds were similar, both having graduated from the same college; they were members of the same church, were reared in more or less the same economic circumstances, and had traveled in the same social circles. Thus it was that a warm friendship developed between the two.

As people everywhere are prone to talk, so it was in Wellington City. As Jane and Carter were seen together more and more, more and more could be heard comments regarding their relationship.

"John and I saw Jane Porter and Carter Wellington at the Steak House last evening," remarked Sally Henry in a conversation with her friends at Byron's Department Store.

"I guess Carter misses his mother terribly," said one. "I don't blame him for seeking companionship. It's a shame when a son becomes so attached to his mother. Inevitably something like this happens."

"Do you think they have serious intentions?" asked Sally.

"Who knows? I don't see anything wrong with their being sweethearts. More power to them both. They are not children anymore."

Such were the comments heard around the town. At the church Jane and Carter could be seen sitting in the same pew during the worship services. Carter would drive Jane to her home while William provided his own transportation, preferring to encourage the younger people to be alone. Often in the afternoon the two would take drives in the country, to the lake, or would visit mutual friends. More and more Carter would invite Jane to a dinner at the most famous restaurant in the area, to attend a play or a musical.

Finally, after an especially romantic evening, Carter drove Jane home and, as was her custom, Jane invited Carter into the house. If William had not yet retired, there would be the usual few words of greeting, after which he would thoughtfully depart to another part of the house.

"What a pleasant evening we have had tonight," Jane said. "The filet mignon was prepared just right and the lemon chiffon pie—I never tasted better. Besides a delicious meal, we were together. Thank you so much!"

"Yes, Jane, I have been thinking the same thing. Wouldn't it be wonderful if you and I could be together for always?"

Jane, appearing to be surprised, said, "What do you mean, Carter?"

"Can't you guess? Are you surprised that I am proposing to you?"

"Not really, I guess. I have been thinking about what I would say if you did."

"Well, what are you going to say?"

Jane lowered her eyelids and her chin. "What do you want me to say?"

"I am hoping you will say 'Yes'."

"Carter, my feelings toward you are as deep as yours are toward me. I have often wondered why good etiquette does not allow a woman to propose to the man she loves. But I must think of Father. I wouldn't want him to have a lonely old age."

"Your father will present no problems at all. Jane, you know that wherever we live your father will live with us. I have learned to love him just as I loved my own father."

"May I have twenty-four hours to think about it and to discuss the matter with Father?"

"As you wish, dear. Goodnight, I'll be running along."

When Carter left Jane, he seemed to have a new spring in his step. As he drove his car into the garage he was humming a tune, something he had not done recently. Life seemed to have a new meaning. Not in so many words, but Jane had practically said she loved him, and he was sure that he loved her. Feeling confident Jane's father would be amenable to the idea of her marrying him, he slept well. At the office the next day his associates noted a change in his manner.

"What makes you so happy today, Carter?" asked his assistant. "Did Jane say 'Yes'?"

"Not yet, but I am hoping she will. In fact, I am expecting it. Women like to keep their men guessing for a while."

Jane related the events of the evening before to her father, including the discussion she and Carter had concerning his future happiness.

William spoke. "I have been wondering when you would be talking to me on that subject. Why don't you and Carter come to live in this house? The Porters and the Wellingtons have always been friends. In fact, good friends. There is room for us all. I have been rehearsing just what I would say when you came to me and said 'Carter proposed to me last night'."

"Yes, Father, I know that's true, but day-in-and-day-out contact is another matter."

"I'm sure we can all get along together. Anyhow, I am not young anymore. I will not always be around. I have been concerned about you for some time and about your future when I am gone."

Jane was saddened at the thought of the day when she would no longer have her father, but happy that he had extended the invitation to Carter and her. As Jane pursued her activities of the day, her friends noticed a certain animation in her manner that had not been present before, just as Carter's friends and associates had noticed the animation in him. That evening Jane was ready to accompany Carter to the theater. It wasn't important what was being shown, they were together. The conversation of the evening before was not mentioned until they returned to Jane's home. After an unusually warm greeting, William vacated the parlor to Jane and Carter.

Carter could hardly wait. What was Jane going to say? He was reasonably sure she was going to say "Yes," but why hadn't she brought up the subject early in the evening? Then Carter asked himself, "Why haven't I mentioned the subject?" Apparently, each was waiting upon the other.

"What do you say, Jane?"

"What do you think I am going to say?"

"I think you are going to say 'Yes'."

"You are right!"

"Let me ask you the traditional question in the traditional manner," insisted Carter, as he dropped to his knees before her. Taking her right hand, and looking squarely into her eyes, he asked, "Will you marry me?" and in the traditional manner, Jane assured him. "Yes," she whispered.

"So it's settled?"

"It is settled. Father has invited us to come to live in this house. I hope that is agreeable with you."

"What could be better? I don't want to live at the Wellington place any longer than I have to. Your father has invited us to live with him. We want to get married. Any place with you is agreeable with me."

With that Carter reached into his pocket. "I purchased this yesterday anticipating your answer. Please let me have your left hand."

Jane extended her trembling right hand, then realizing her mistake, she quickly withdrew it and extended the left one. Carter selected the third finger and pushed the brilliant solitaire on it.

"This makes it official," as he embraced her and gave her a long, tender kiss. "You are mine now," he said as soon as he could recover his breath.

31

"Carter, how lovely!" Jane said excitedly as she gazed at the magnificence on her finger. "And it just fits! How did you know the size?"

"Why, before I presented you with my mother's dinner ring last month I took it to Brighton's Jewelry to have it cleaned and polished and I had Henry measure the size. I tried it on the third finger of your left hand, you will remember, and it fit exactly. When you protested that you would be wearing it on the third finger of your right hand, I found it would fit that finger, too. I guess, even then, you wanted to save the lefthand finger for another ring. Right?"

"Maybe," said Jane.

Jane was not wearing the beautiful topaz ring that night because she felt it was too lovely and had too much sentimentality attached to it to wear it except upon very special dressed-up occasions. Carter's father had presented the ring to his mother as a birthday gift soon after they were married. Carter had become so fond of Jane that he had wanted her to have the ring, anticipating even then that someday she would be his wife.

Jane sat on the sofa close to Carter with her hand resting on his, admiring the beautiful stone set in an equally beautiful mounting. When she was able to speak again, Jane expressed her heartfelt thanks. Then she said, "I wonder if Father is still up." But when he did not answer a light tap on the door to his room, she concluded he had already gone to bed and was asleep.

"I will have to wait until tomorrow to show him. Carter, you'd better go. I just want some time to revel in my happiness. What time will you be coming tomorrow evening? We must talk about our wedding plans."

"Oh, I guess the usual time. Or do you want to have dinner at the Steak House?"

"No, I don't think so. Let me prepare a dinner for you. I want to show you that my culinary arts are not altogether lacking. What would you like? To eat, I mean."

"Let me be surprised. Make it early. I'll be anxious," requested Carter.

With that he kissed her again and took his leave.

5.

CARTER'S ECSTASY KNEW NO bounds. As he drove home he began to make his future plans. "What will I do with my house—the house known as 'The Wellington Place' for so many generations?" Even though he no longer wanted to live there, it pained him to think that no longer would it be occupied by a Wellington. He would have to talk it over with Jane.

Jane arose early the next morning after a sleepless night. She wanted her father to be the first to know about the ring.

"It seems but yesterday," he said, "that you were entering college. In fact, it seems such a short time ago that you were born! The years pass so quickly. I am happy for you. Now I have no fear about your happiness after I am gone. I will be proud to have Carter Wellington as a son-in-law."

Jane was alone after her father departed for his office at the factory. She sat at the breakfast table for a long while thinking about her plans, which, of course would be discussed with Carter. "When will the wedding take place? What will Carter do with his house? I hope he doesn't dispose of those priceless antiques. But how would all the pieces fit into this house?"

After an hour or two she came back to reality. She began to make plans for the evening meal. Until Carter came into her life, she and her father dined most evenings together. Rosie, their faithful cook and housekeeper, was always on time with her tempting preparations. Jane thought, "Can I ever match her skill in this respect?" But then she thought, "It will probably never be necessary. Rosie will always be here." But for this one evening Jane wanted to try. Jane sometimes wished she had been reared in a less affluent home without benefit of maids or cooks.

Because of her frequent associations with Carter, Jane had learned that he was a man of simple tastes in food. She sent Rosie to the market to purchase enough of the best pork chops available. Most of the items Jane would need for a tasty meal were already in Rosie's well-stocked pantry.

With some assistance from Rosie, Jane prepared a delicious meal, and she felt proud of the results. She took great pains in setting the table for two in the small dining room where she and her father usually took the evening meal. The large main dining room was reserved for large crowds, and Jane thought Carter and she would both appreciate the coziness of the smaller room. Jane had learned the art of entertaining from her mother and she knew just how to place the forks, spoons, knives, drinking glasses, and napkins beside the dinner plates—all set on a cloth of white lace. A white, lighted candle set in a silver candlestick added the final touch.

As Carter arrived and beheld Jane at the door, dressed in a long flowered skirt and white blouse, he believed that he had never seen her so beautiful.

"Hello, darling," he said, as he stooped slightly to kiss her. "How beautiful you are!" Of course, he had often admired her appearance, but tonight she seemed even more attractive to him.

"Dinner is ready. Come into the dining room."

At sight of the beautiful table and the even more beautiful woman standing beside it, the features of her face enhanced by the glow of the candle, Carter thought, "This must be heaven!" As he pulled Jane's chair out from the table for her to sit, he kissed her again. He had never been so happy. The same could have been said of Jane. After Carter was seated on her left, according to their custom, they bowed their heads to thank God for the good things of life.

"I remembered one of your favorites is pork chops," said Jane. "I must learn your likes and dislikes in food, but we have taken so many meals together, I should already know."

"Anything you prepare I am bound to like."

"You say that now, but will you still be saying it twenty years from now?"

"I am sure I will, dear."

When dinner was finished, the two went to the parlor to talk.

"Let's talk about our wedding plans," Jane suggested.

"That sounds like a good subject of conversation. But first, I want to compliment you on the fine meal. Did you do it all alone?"

"I must confess I had some assistance from Rosie."

"No restaurant could have done it nearly as well. But wasn't it a lot of hard work?"

"A little, but I wanted to do it just for you."

"Thank you so much! Now, for some serious conversation," Carter began. "When do you wish the wedding to take place, dear?"

"Well, this is late August. As you well know, it will require some time to organize a wedding party, engage musicians, including a soloist, the church, the minister and a host of other details. Too, the dressmaker will need time to make my gown and those of the bridesmaids."

"How much time do you think all this will take?" asked Carter.

"You might be surprised at the amount of time all these things require. Then, too, propriety dictates that the wedding not take place too soon after the engagement is announced."

"You still haven't answered my question," remonstrated Carter.

"I really don't know what to say. I suppose you are anxious that we have the wedding as soon as possible."

"Of course I am, dear," assured Carter.

"Also," Jane further commented, "before we set the date we should think about where we want to go for the honeymoon. If we go to a warm climate, we would want the wedding in the winter. That is something we haven't talked about yet. Oh dear, there are so many things to decide. Also, we should announce our engagement formally. Not that everybody won't know anyhow when I start going around town wearing this diamond."

"Have you thought about where we should spend our honeymoon?" queried Carter.

"Oh," said Jane, "there are many interesting places. Since it will be at least approaching winter, we should seek out a warm climate. I used to think as a little girl I would like to take a trip on an ocean vessel if I ever had the good fortune to become a bride and go on a honeymoon."

"Well, let's decide. How does a Caribbean cruise sound to you? We could spend about three weeks on a cruise. The wedding could be immediately after Thanksgiving. That way, we could spend Thanksgiving with your father and be back by the Christmas holidays. How does that sound to you?"

"Oh, that would be great! Carter, you are so thoughtful of my father."

"That would give us both time to get all the details attended to. But, shucks! That's a long time yet."

If we don't have the wedding immediately after Thanksgiving, it would be better to wait until even later. Folks are always so absorbed with their families during December, and anyhow I wouldn't like abandoning father to spend the holidays alone."

"In that event, I guess we had better plan the wedding the Saturday following Thanksgiving. Agreed?"

"Agreed," replied Jane.

With that, Carter arose, announcing his departure and kissing Jane good night.

When Jane explained the wedding plans to her father the following day, he said, "Very well. You prepare the engagement announcements. We'll send some out to a few friends and relatives."

The engraved message read:

Mr. William Porter announces the engagement of his daughter, Jane Elizabeth, to Mr. James Carter Wellington.

A late fall wedding is planned.

On Sunday, the next day, Jane and Carter sat together in the church service as usual. While the worshipers were assembling, Lucy Bates whispered to her husband, John, "Do you see what I see? Jane Porter is wearing a diamond that knocks your eyes out. I have been wondering when it would show up."

"Well, you women notice everything, don't you?—except holes in their husbands' socks. I put on three pairs this morning before I found a pair without a hole in at least one sock."

"Oh, finally, Banker Wellington has bought Jane a diamond.

It certainly took him long enough," said another worshiper.

Such buzzings could be heard after the service among the many who had noticed the ring.

No one yet had the courage to talk to Jane and Carter about the latest event in their lives. During the following week the engagement announcements had been mailed to certain friends and relatives, many of whom were church members. On Sunday, Pastor Mitchell read his copy of the announcement from the pulpit; also the notice was published in the weekly church bulletin mailed to each member. Of course, such an event in the lives of two members of Wellington City society would also be published in the *Wellington City Courier*. So, the engagement of Jane Porter and J. Carter Wellington did not remain a secret for many days, nor was it a great surprise to the townsfolk in general.

Genevieve Thornton and Gladys Hayes were chatting on the street a few days later.

"What do you think of the latest news?" asked Genevieve.

"What news is that?"

"About Jane Porter and Carter Wellington, of course," replied Genevieve.

"Oh, that! Oh, I'm not greatly surprised. They each need someone. I don't blame them. I think they will make a good pair. Carter has already come by a wad of dough and Jane is in line for one. I suppose no expense will be spared in putting on the biggest celebration you ever heard of for the wedding."

"Do you think there will be any heirs?" questioned practical Genevieve. Without waiting for a reply, she went on, "You know she is already in the middle thirties and he must be forty or more."

Gladys commented, "Well, it's not unheard of for a woman to have her first child at that age or even older, but it's rather unusual. My mother was thirty-nine when I was born, but, of course, I was her fourth child. Makes a difference, but my next oldest sister is fourteen years older than I am."

Genevieve recalled, "I knew a couple before I was married who had their first child when she was thirty-seven. The child never was quite right. He grew to manhood, though, and was able to get along in the world. The woman's second child, born

37

two years later, was normal. You never know!"

"Where do you think they will live? In the Wellington house, with old man Porter, or elsewhere?" asked Gladys.

"Rumor has it that the couple will live in the Porter house with Jane's father. If that is true, I suppose Wellington will dispose of the old place. He never liked it anyhow, since his mother passed away. Without a Wellington in that place, the town won't be the same. But change is always taking place. Well, Gladys, I must go. Paul will be home soon for supper."

Such were the comments heard around about town concerning the engagement and forthcoming marriage. Although Jane and Carter were aware of and expected such observations and comments, the couple was not disturbed by them.

Both Jane and Carter were busily occupied with many details, not the least of which for Jane was her gown which, once selected, required numerous trips to the dressmaker for fittings. Besides her own, the gowns for her four bridesmaids, maid of honor, and a flower girl had to be selected and made. Also, arrangements had to be made for the rental of appropriate outfits for her father and the ring bearer. Since Wellington City had no source of supply for such things, it was necessary to travel to Erie for these items. Engaging the church and Pastor Mitchell, the reception room at Wellington City's best hotel, as well as arranging for the serving of food to the guests, mailing invitations and a host of other items too numerous to mention, kept Jane in a flurry of excitement, near physical and mental exhaustion for the months and weeks preceding the wedding.

As for Carter, he too had some responsibilities to think about. He was busy arranging the details of the honeymoon trip, the customary rehearsal dinner for the wedding party, closing up of the old homestead, selecting the best man who, happily, would attend to the providing of appropriate clothing for the groom. Then, too, he could not forget nor neglect frequent evenings with Jane.

Somehow, every detail had been completed, except one—the rehearsal. Each member of the wedding party gathered at the church for last minute instructions and to go through the routine for the following day. Finally, all appeared to be set for a beautiful and well-managed ceremony. The late ,evening rehearsal dinner took place at the finest restaurant in Wellington City where members of the party joked with Carter and reminded him that this was his last night as a free man.

Photographs of the bridal party had been taken and at exactly two o'clock on the big day, Jane, nervous and exhausted yet happy, stood in the vestibule of the old church. The guests had all been seated in their appropriate pews. With Jane were her bridesmaids, maid of honor, her father, and the ushers. Miss Bryant, the organist, had been playing the instrument softly. At the sound of the right chord, the ushers proceeded down the aisle to their places, followed by the bridesmaids one by one, the maid of honor, and the flower girl. At the proper distance, Jane, holding her bouquet of white flowers, proceeded down the aisle on the arm of her father. Waiting at the foot of the chancel steps, with Pastor Mitchell, Carter approached Jane, who extended her right hand toward him. The ceremony began:

"Who giveth this woman . . . . " read Pastor Mitchell from his little black book, to which William properly replied, "I do."

"James Carter Wellington," the ceremony continued, "do you take this woman . . . . "

"I do," responded Carter.

"Jane Elizabeth Porter, do you take this man . . . . "

"I do," whispered Jane, inaudible to all except those within the immediate vicinity.

As the double-ring ceremony was completed, the maid of honor lifted Jane's veil for the traditional kiss from the groom, the organ began the processional and bride and groom hurried down the aisle, followed by other members of the wedding party. On the church steps, the rice was not spared; nor had the old shoes, tin cans, and the like attached to their car been forgotten by well-wishing friends.

At the reception immediately following, Jane and Carter took their place in the receiving line where they were wished the best by those present. Later, Jane cut the elaborate cake and shared the first piece with Carter.

Jane and Carter departed early from the reception to change to travel clothing and to board the evening train to New York where, after relaxing overnight, they would embark on the cruise ship for the Caribbean. Once alone in their suite on the

39

train, they breathed a sigh of relief. They watched the moonlit countryside move by them and talked until they made their way to the dining car. Since they were not hungry, they ordered only tea and wafers. Then, returning to their suite, which had been prepared for the night by the competent porter while they were in the dining car, they retired for the night. Tired as they were, they slept only fitfully. Carter arose early and dressed quickly while Jane, as women do, dallied a while longer. After a leisurely breakfast in the diner, the train soon arrived at the terminal from which they were whisked to their hotel by taxi. The remainder of that day and a part of the following day was spent relaxing, for the most part, in the luxury of the hotel. At noon on the second day, they departed for the pier where they boarded the luxury cruiser. For the next few weeks they were to experience the happiest time of their lives thus far, enjoying the swimming pool, the luxurious dining and ballrooms, the decks, the ports of call, the pleasant salt air – and each other.

6.

A GENTLE SNOW WAS FALLING as Carter and Jane Wellington alighted from the train at Wellington City in midmorning a few days before Christmas. Their honeymoon voyage had ended, but the air of expectancy had not. William was waiting with his car to carry the couple and their luggage to the house that would now be Carter's home as well as Jane's. Within the confines of the traveling bags were many souvenirs and momentoes of the various places the couple had visited, to serve as reminders of the exciting journey.

After the welcoming kisses, hugs, and handshakes, the excited group found themselves at home where Jane, the interesting and animated speaker that she was, related the highlights of the trip. She would be recalling many of the details for weeks to come. Carter relived the moments again with his wife and often added an interesting detail that Jane had omitted. Many of the same events were recounted to their friends on the following Wednesday at Family Night.

"Did you take photographs?" asked many of their friends.

"Oh, yes, many," replied Jane.

"Oh, you must show them to us sometime!"

Thus, the honeymoon voyage of Jane and Carter Wellington was not forgotten soon by their friends, and never by the happy couple.

At the beginning of January, Carter again resumed the active command of business at the bank. Meanwhile, William could be found daily at the factory and Jane took charge of affairs of the household with the able help of faithful Rosie. Jane and Carter had moved into the large bedroom heretofore reserved for guests. Jane's former room, smaller yet still commodious, became the guest room.

Carter, not willing to show a lack of appreciation for Ellen who had served his household for so many years, presented her with a generous gift and told her of a new position that was available to her with the family of one of the officers of the bank, Mr. Johns. As Carter handed the envelope to Ellen, he said, "Ellen, you have been with us these many years; in fact, I can't remember when you were not here. This conveys only a very small part of my appreciation for not only your faithful service but for your loyalty throughout the years. You have seemed as one of us. Nothing material can ever fully repay you for the years you have spent with the Wellingtons, but I hope the contents of this envelope will help."

Ellen was speechless for the moment, but the tears in her eyes revealed her emotions.

Carter assured her that the Johns family was a very fine one and that if she chose to accept the position she would be well satisfied. But if she did encounter any problems or difficulties, she had only to let him know.

When Ellen recovered her composure, she expressed her joy that her former employer had found happiness and thanked him for all of his kindnesses. As for the new position, she asked Carter to arrange a visit for her with the new family.

"Were it not for the fact that I am without a home, I would retire. But where would I go? The old folks home? God forbid! I want to be around young folks! I'm only in the early sixties. If the good Lord wills, I can serve a good family many years yet. The Wellingtons are the only family I have worked for since I became a widow in my youth. You folks have given me a good home and something to live for."

The tears came to Carter's eyes for the first time since his mother's death.

"Ellen, I hope you will not forget to visit Jane and me whenever you can."

Carter then visited the home of Bill Smithson to present him with a token of appreciation. The old handyman accepted the envelope with emotion but, being a male, exhibited more restraint than had Ellen.

"Bill, you know, of course, that I will be living at the Porters, but I have not yet decided what I will do with the old family home. While I am deciding, it will be closed and unoccupied. Jane and I will want to move some of the pieces of furniture to our new home. But most will remain just as they are for the time being. I want you to continue taking care of things each day just as you have in the past, understand?"

"Yes, Mr. Wellington, but it won't be the same."

Then Carter continued, "I suppose the sensible course of action would be to sell the property, but I find it hard to bring myself to do that. I was born there as you well know, and it has always been home to me, until Mother left us. Then it became only a place to sleep, keep my clothing, and once in a while, to take a meal."

"I understand how you feel, Mr. Wellington, and I can't say that I blame you, but life must go on and I'm sure you will be much happier now, even in spite of the memories."

"Thank you, Bill!" The two shook hands and Carter returned home to eat the dinner which Rosie had waiting for him and Jane.

Carter and Jane visited the old Wellington homestead and, together, they selected such objects as the old cherry bureau which had been in the family since Carter's grandfather's day. They also chose the old tall hallway clock, with its long pendulum swinging almost constantly for as long as Carter could remember.

"Oh, how I wish we could use many of these other pieces too," lamented Jane. "Your grandmother Carter's massive dining-room suite that your mother inherited. How old is it? What workmanship! Oh yes, we must have the portrait in oil of your mother as a young woman. Who did you say did it? We can hang it in our room. Of course, Father has many lovely old pieces too, but I wouldn't want to ask him to part with anything that he doesn't want to. The heirlooms of two families create quite a problem when it comes to making choices, doesn't it? Let's not disturb the remainder until I have had time to talk to Father. Perhaps there are some items that Father does not particularly care to keep."

"That's a good idea," agreed Carter. "We don't have to decide everything today."

Jane and Carter had an interesting time planning the

arrangement of the additional furniture. Together they discussed the placing of other items should they decide to bring any of them to their present home.

Competition in the manufacture of chairs was becoming ever more keen and William Porter found, despite his age, that it was necessary for him to spend more and more time in his office.

One day he addressed Carter, "Carter, I am not young anymore, as I have reminded you many times. The business is requiring more and more of my time. How about you and Jane assuming the duties of managing the household? I will become what you might call "a boarder."

"But Father," as Carter had become accustomed to addressing him, "we don't believe you should be pushed out of your own house! We can't permit you to become a mere boarder in your own home!"

"I am not being pushed out! I will be glad to be relieved of the responsibility. Anyhow, I will still be here. You can't get rid of me entirely, even if you wanted to," he joked. "I will still maintain my room upstairs."

"What's all the discussion about?" Jane asked as she came upon the scene.

"Oh, Father thinks he is too old and too busy to be concerned about the affairs of the house," Carter answered.

"Perhaps too busy, but not too old. You are just as capable as you ever were!" admonished Jane. "What do you want to be, only a boarder here?"

"That is what I proposed to your dear husband."

"Well," responded Jane. "whatever you want to call yourself, you will always be one of us."

"I'm serious, Jane. You and Carter can take over the management of the household affairs. Just let me live here."

"Well, Father, if that is what you want. Carter and I can see that the place is maintained, the bills paid, and so on. But it will always be your home, too! Understand that!"

"I understand," answered William. "I will really enjoy the freedom."

Soon the Wellington family, Carter and Jane together with William, became accustomed to their new living arrangements and enjoyed a happy family relationship.

One evening, upon retiring, Jane and Carter were talking. "Everything here is perfect except for one thing, darling."

"What is that?" Carter asked solicitously.

"I wonder if God will bless us with children as He has most other couples. Of course, we are older, but do you think we are too old to properly rear children? Do you think I am too old to become a mother?"

"Don't be discouraged, sweetheart," comforted Carter. "We have been married only two months. Let's be patient."

After a few weeks Jane began to experience curious sensations within herself. Upon relating the strange symptoms to Carter he elatedly exclaimed, "Oh, perhaps we are to become parents after all. Let's make an appointment with Dr. Franklin."

After a routine examination the next week, Dr. Franklin advised them, "It is my opinion that you are pregnant, Jane. I can't be quite sure this early, but that is my judgment."

Dr. Franklin continued his conversation with the thrilled couple. "How old are you, Jane?"

Jane was not reluctant to reveal her age to Dr. Franklin. "I will be thirty-six in a few weeks."

"Of course, as you no doubt are aware, thirty-six is not the usual age for a first child. The chances of a normal pregnancy are not as great as in younger women. Yet, in my experience, many women your age do have a normal pregnancy and deliver a normal child."

"Yes, I am aware of the risk," responded Jane.

Dr. Franklin continued, "Fortunately, we now have a physician in town who specializes in obstetrics and gynecology. He comes highly recommended in his field, especially in those cases where there is more than the usual possibility of a difficult pregnancy. I am referring to Dr. James Sullivan. With your permission, I will arrange an appointment with him for you. I would strongly recommend that course of action."

Almost in unison, Jane and Carter replied, "By all means."

Dr. Sullivan verified the diagnosis of their family physician. "Yes, all indications are that you are pregnant, Jane. But I see no real reason for alarm. I will expect you to see me each month, or more often if you feel it is necessary, until the eighth month, then every week. With good prenatal care, all should go well."

Thus it appeared that God was about to answer Jane and Carter's petition.

Jane and Carter revealed the happy news to Jane's father. William appeared even more elated than the prospective parents. "Me, William Porter, a grandfather? Who could have ever thought such a thing would happen? Now I can be content that neither the Porter nor the Wellington families will become extinct. For a while I was somewhat concerned."

Soon all Wellington City was more or less surprised to learn of the expected arrival of an heir at the Wellington household. Jane and Carter could scarcely contain their happiness. But yet, did they dare expect too much? They could not allow themselves to entertain thoughts of the possibility of other than a normal delivery of a normal child. At last, the J. Carter Wellingtons became the proud parents of a son which had already been named "William" for his grandfather Porter, and "Carter" for his father — William Carter Wellington. The avalanche of gifts that came to the home from well-wishing friends and relatives was sufficient that had triplets arrived, there would have been no lack of outfits or conveniences for the new mother and children.

As the apparently healthy and robust child developed and began to acquire normal physical abilities, the Wellingtons began to long for another child. But it was not to be and William remained their only child. Yet Jane and Carter were grateful that they had been permitted to become the parents of even one child.

The grandfather, called "Father" by both Jane and Carter and "Mr. Porter" by Rosie and others to avoid confusion by the presence of two Williams in the home, was later referred to as "Grandpa" for the child's benefit.

As the child William developed his physical abilities, one aspect of his development seemed to lag behind — that of speech.

One day Jane expressed her concern. "Why can't William say anything except 'Mommy' or 'Daddy'? Mostly, he utters only unintelligible sounds. He will soon be three years old!" she said to Carter.

Carter replied, "Oh, perhaps he is just a little slow. I am sure he will be okay."

Later, after William had observed his third birthday, Jane was discussing William's apparent slowness of speech. "Rosie," Jane said, "I'm very concerned about William's slowness in learning to talk. He is three now and should be doing much better, despite your constant insistence that everything is all right."

"But, Mrs. Wellington, you must remember that he is with adults and not children his own age, which makes a big difference," answered Rosie, trying to calm the mother's fears, even though the older woman was herself fearful.

That same evening, Jane came to grips with the problem. "Carter, we must seek some professional advice. Don't you think so?"

"Well, I don't know whether we need be so concerned or not, but if it will make you happier I will be glad to make arrangements for a thorough professional analysis of the child's capabilities."

The next day, Carter called Dr. Franklin and related his and Jane's concerns, asking his opinion and questioning the possibility of recommending a specialist in the field. Dr. Franklin assured Carter that he was not greatly alarmed and further explained that Wellington City had no such specialist. However, he could recommend both a child psychologist and speech therapist in Erie and he further volunteered to secure an appointment for an examination of the child.

Later the same day, Dr. Franklin called Carter at the bank. "Carter, I have been able to get an appointment for next Tuesday at 10 A.M. with Dr. John Stevens in Erie, if that is satisfactory with you. I know Dr. Stevens is an outstanding child psychologist."

Carter assured Dr. Franklin that he and Jane would visit the specialist with their son at the appointed time. "Dr. Franklin," Carter further added, "I don't know what Jane and I would do without you!"

"Oh, it's nothing, Carter. I'm always glad to help where I can."

On Tuesday the Wellington family journeyed to Erie for the first of what proved to be a series of six consultations, tests, and examinations. Finally, Dr. Wasson, the director of the speech clinic, and Dr. Stevens conferred with the Wellingtons. Both men were in agreement as to the results of the tests.

"Mr. and Mrs. Wellington," declared Stevens, "to be sure, your son is a little backward in his speech progress, but I do not find anything seriously wrong with his mental capacity. His measurable I.Q. seems to be within normal limits and his physical dexterity is superb. He appears to have no physical speech impairment. I am inclined to believe that the absence of other children may be a factor in his development. At any rate, at this point, I do not believe you have undue reason for alarm. Some children simply require more time than others. If I can be of further help, or if further problems develop, please get in touch with me."

Dr. Stevens and Dr. Wasson bid the family good-bye and the consultation was thus concluded. The family returned home considerably relieved. During the next years before entering school, William did show some improvement, although the parents were never entirely free from apprehension. However, the constant assurances of close family friends were of some comfort. In the absence of nursery schools as such in Wellington City, Jane and Carter made a special effort to bring William into frequent contact with other children, through church activities, at children's playgrounds, and such other opportunities as might present themselves. Friends assured the parents that once William was enrolled in school, a great improvement would be seen. Since Wellington City had not thus far felt the need of the luxury of a kindergarten, its children were required to await their sixth birthday before beginning their formal education.

7.

J. CARTER WELLINGTON, being a civic-minded citizen, had taken an extracurricular interest in the affairs of the community, as many businessmen have always done. He had served as both member, and later, president, of the school board of Wellington City. His dominant personality, his keen business aptitude, his more than usual interest in the schools, and his many years of service had merited him, by mutual agreement of the other members of the board, the title of almost a one-man board of directors. It was a responsibility which Carter did not regard lightly. The school authorities had long since learned that with J. Carter Wellington at the helm of the board, they could not rule the schools with a free hand. J. Carter had been a watchdog, so to speak, of their activities, ranging from supervising the hiring of teaching personnel and financial accounting to the formulation of the curriculum itself, a record he had regarded with great pride.

Carter, Jane, and their son had looked ahead with anticipation to September when William, who had become known as "Bill," would enter the first grade. Although showing marked improvement in his speaking abilities, he had not yet reached, even closely, the level of his peers. The three had talked about the day he would start school for many weeks. One morning when Jane awakened Bill, he said excitedly, "Is today me go to school?"

"You mean, 'Is this the day I go to school?'"

Bill repeated after her, "Is this the day me go to school?"

"No! No! 'Is this the day I go to school?' "

Upon the third attempt, the boy used the correct words, but past experience in coaching him indicated he would repeat the error many times.

49

"No, dear, we are having a picnic with some other children in the park."

Bill found much pleasure in being with other children, although at times they were cruel to him by attempting to avoid him, or referring to him as a baby or being tongue-tied. This sort of treatment caused Bill to cry and disturbed Jane, but she considered it important that he associate with children his own age.

Finally, the day arrived—Bill's first day of school. Jane aroused him early and dressed him in the clothing of his choice, a red outfit that enhanced his dark curly hair. He and Jane walked the three blocks together. Jane and Bill had visited the school twice during the past weeks in order to acquaint him with the location of his classroom.

As Bill and his mother climbed the four or five steps to the front door, Bill very proudly exclaimed, "Me know my room. Me take you."

"Okay. You show me," answered Jane without mentioning his error. "Pretend I don't know where it is!"

Bill very ably lead the way down a long hall. He stopped at the first-grade room where his teacher, Miss Kerr, was standing just inside. Several other children, who would be Bill's classmates, had already assembled and were talking and giggling among themselves. Miss Kerr and Jane needed no introduction. The young woman had lived in the vicinity of Wellington City since her birth.

"Hello, Miss Kerr," Jane said. Although Jane was well enough acquainted with the young woman to have appropriately addressed her by her first name, she used the surname for Bill's benefit. "You have met my son, William, I believe. You know Miss Kerr, don't you, Bill?"

Bill nodded.

"Oh, yes!" Thelma Kerr replied. "I am sure we will get along just fine."

Miss Kerr reminded Jane that school on the first day would be in session for only a few hours—just to become acquainted, to assign the pupils their seats, and to issue the list of books they would need, and that the children would be ready to leave for home at noon.

"Thank you, Miss Kerr. I shall be here at five minutes to

twelve for him. Good-bye, Bill," said Jane, as she stooped to kiss him. "Miss Kerr will show you what you are to do."

" 'Bye, Mamma!"

Jane left the room and walked down the hall and out the door alone, finding it difficult to fight back the tears in her eyes.

"He's a good boy," she thought, wondering how he would be accepted by the other children and how well he would mix with them.

Thelma Kerr had grown up on a small subsistence farm. One of eight children in a family which had always lived near the poverty level, Thelma was the only child who had finished high school, over the objections of her parents. They had felt that children, especially girls, should help at home as soon as they became old enough to leave school. Yet Thelma had been valedictorian of her graduating class, and after graduation, she secured employment as a sales clerk in a retail store in Wellington City. She saved almost every cent of her wages, walking to and from work. When fall came, even though her employer was sad that his competent employee was leaving, she entered the state university. Using her savings and a scholarship, together with summer employment, she managed to graduate four years later without asking aid from her parents, near the top of her class, with a degree in elementary education.

Now beginning her third year in the classroom, Thelma was anxious that her achievements be recognized by the school authorities in order that she be accorded permanent tenure in accordance with the current policy of the Wellington City school system. Already vaguely aware of William Wellington's problem, and also aware that the boy's father was president of the school board and influential in the granting of tenure, Thelma was extremely interested in seeing that the child be recognized and helped in every way possible. But yet she had more than twenty other children to teach, too.

Thelma soon discovered that William was not even the student she had expected. She had anticipated a slow but diligent pupil. With the latter quality she was satisfied, even pleased, but she had not expected that the child would be totally unable to cope with the assignments given the other children.

The situation was disconcerting to Thelma. Aside from

51

feeling sadness at the inability of any child to learn, she was particularly distressed that she was unable to help the child whose father was the president and the chief moving force on the school board.

"What effect will this inability have on the granting of my permanent tenure at the end of the school year?" she contemplated. "I wonder if Mr. Wellington realizes the extent of his son's incapacity?"

After a few weeks, Thelma called the Wellington home. Jane answered the telephone. Thelma hardly knew how to begin the conversation. After the usual pleasantries, she commented upon Bill's good behavior and his diligent application. Then she said, "I am wondering if you would mind if I keep Bill for about an hour after school each evening for a few weeks. He needs some special attention which I can't give during school hours."

Jane, of course, was aware that Bill would likely find it difficult to compete with his classmates, but she had never discussed the problem with his teacher.

"Why, yes, if it is necessary. Or perhaps you could give his assignment to me and I could help him."

"That would be good, but I really believe he should be under the supervision of a person who has been trained to teach young children."

"When do you want to begin the special lessons?"

"I believe we should start right away, so that he will not fall behind. Suppose we start Monday evening of next week."

"Very well," said Jane. "I will delay calling for him until one hour after school closes, beginning Monday."

Jane thus reluctantly agreed to what amounted to Bill being singled out as a child needing special help. She was greatly pained that Bill's inadequacies were now known to other than their close circle of friends.

Weeks passed. Jane and Carter had been faithful in cooperating with Thelma, both at school and at home. But Bill showed little improvement. The situation was desperate! Finally, Thelma approached the school principal.

"Mr. Osgood," she began, "I have a child in my classroom—a child from a prominent family—who apparently is unable to learn. You no doubt are acquainted with the parents. As you probably have already guessed, I am speaking of the Wellington boy. As you also already know, I have been taking an hour or so after school each day for several weeks to give Bill special help. But he has grasped very little, either in the classroom or as an individual student. You are also well aware that J. Carter Wellington is not only the president of the school board, but practically the whole board itself. If he is not satisfied with my performance, he may cause me trouble when my permanent tenure is due at the end of this year!"

Mr. Osgood listened attentively. "Miss Kerr, I can understand your problem. Perhaps one or two of the older teachers would have some ideas as to how to handle a situation of this kind. Shall we give it a try?"

"Yes, please do, Mr. Osgood. It would mean a lot to me if, somehow, we could overcome the difficulty."

"Suppose, then, that I see Miss Lance or Miss Wells about the problem. They have had many years' experience in the schoolroom. I am sure they have been faced with a situation of this kind in the past."

During their free time, the two older teachers attempted to motivate the child by the latest tested methods of teaching, but little progress was made. It was obvious to them by this time that the child was definitely handicapped.

At length, the dreaded truth had to be revealed to the parents who, up to this time, had been encouraged by vague commendations of William's progress. Mr. Osgood, not in an enviable position, took the matter to the superintendent of schools, Mr. Grant Chase. The only suggestion Mr. Chase could provide at this point was continued effort along the same lines as had been practiced in the past weeks.

Since the prolonged effort produced no improvement, Mr. Chase realized something must be done: the parents must be told, come what would, and he should be the one to do it. Superintendent Chase felt that placing the child in an ungraded class, or enrolling the boy in a psychological program would serve no purpose, even if such classes or programs existed in Wellington City or another nearby location. Another approach to the dilemma must be found.

At the time Superintendent Chase brought his family to

Wellington City six years earlier, he had purchased the old Wellington homestead through financing from the Wellington City Bank. Mr. Chase had enjoyed a good business relationship, but never a close social one, with J. Carter Wellington. At times, due to the heavy financial responsibilities of a large family, including two children in college, Mr. Chase had found it difficult to meet the monthly mortgage payments on the house and even though he had fallen somewhat in arrears on occasion, bank personnel had not made an issue of the defaults. To approach J. Carter Wellington, the president, on the delicate subject of the mental deficiencies of his only son and heir apparent, called for extreme tactfulness, if the good business relationship between them were to continue.

After much meditation, Superintendent Chase, the resourceful person that he was, determined a course of action. To protect his teaching staff, he chose to assume full responsibility in the matter. He phoned Mr. Wellington for an appointment.

When the superintendent arrived at the bank he was ushered into the president's office.

"What can Mr. Chase want to discuss?" Carter asked himself. "Is he about to give up the house?" If Carter thought he might wish to speak to him about his son, he pushed the thought aside.

"Could we have the door closed?" asked Mr. Chase.

"Yes, of course," and Carter suited the action to the word.

"Mr. Wellington, I wish to speak to you about your son," Mr. Chase began. "It is not usual that the superintendent of schools speaks directly to the parents about student problems. But Miss Kerr, his teacher, has advised me, through her school principal, of the situation in regard to your child."

After a moment of silence, during which Mr. Chase searched for the right words, he continued. "To put it simply, William is unable to perform first-grade work while in the classroom with the other children." The superintendent, not wishing to incur ill feelings between himself and Carter, had softened the blow by describing the situation less critically than it really was.

He continued, "Miss Kerr is a dedicated teacher and as soon as she became aware of these circumstances, she requested and received permission from you and your wife to keep William for a while after school in order that she might work with him individually. As she expected, William became a good student while working on a one-to-one basis. But back in the classroom he regressed to the previous state. After several attempts at private lessons and then rejoining his classmates, the problem was still present.

"Finally, Miss Kerr consulted her principal, Mr. Osgood, who suggested the cooperation of two of the older teachers. When they were faced with the same results, Mr. Osgood came to me with the problem. Not wishing to merely accept the word of others, I ordered the experiment repeated and William's written work, both in and out of the classroom, submitted to me for inspection. There was no comparison between the work done in the classroom and that done outside."

Mr. Wellington interrupted Superintendent Chase. "Do you happen to have any of William's written work with you?" he asked.

Mr. Chase, not expecting to be pinned down, stammered, "No . . . I'm sorry, I did not retain any of his work in my file. I returned it all to Miss Kerr!"

The two men each attempted to mislead the other: Carter was not willing to admit his son had a problem, and Mr. Chase did not wish to reveal the terrible truth.

As the conference continued, Mr. Chase assured William's father that the situation was not hopeless, that it was not unique, especially in the case of an only child. Other children were apt to distract him.

"But William has always enjoyed the company of other children in the past," observed Carter.

"Yes, perhaps, but attitudes of children do change for inexplicable reasons. This sudden fright is known as "freezing," when a child is unable to perform in competitive situations."

"I am surprised to learn of all this, Mr. Chase! What do you suggest, or what do you recommend that we do?"

"Since William obviously cannot perform just now in the classroom, but is quite competent as an individual student, I would suggest a private tutor for the remainder of the term. There is a strong probability that he will be able to return to the classroom at the beginning of the second grade.

"The Wellington name has been one of respect and achievement throughout the years, and I am sure you want your son to follow in that tradition," Mr. Chase continued. "Your college, New Exeter, can no doubt recommend and put you in touch with a good tutor, someone with the qualities William needs, such as confidence in the child and dedication. Perhaps you can arrange for the tutor to live in your home to enable her to observe William's total environment. In order that your son may be considered a regularly enrolled student in our school system, I would also suggest the tutor be accorded an honorary teaching status. The child would use the same course of study as that used in the school. He would be ready for the second grade at the same time as his classmates when he re-enters the classroom. Do you think Mrs. Wellington would be agreeable to the plan I have outlined?"

Carter Wellington's delayed response, for what seemed to Mr. Chase an eternity, was embarrassing. "Isn't he going to reply to my comments?" Mr. Chase was beginning to wonder.

Finally Carter responded, "Naturally, I feel very keenly my disappointment in the boy as I am sure his mother will when she learns of the matter. However, in consideration of the great effort put forth in William's behalf and the unusual interest that has been shown, not only by Miss Kerr and Mr. Osgood, but especially by you, to give you less than our full cooperation would indeed be ungrateful. I will discuss the matter with Mrs. Wellington this very evening. Personally, on the face of it, I feel that your plan appears to be well thought out and a practical one. I am sure Mrs. Wellington will agree with me."

With that, Mr. Chase thanked Carter for his time and took his leave. As he traveled back to his office, he was satisfied that he had convinced Mr. Wellington that William really was a good student outside the classroom without endangering their relationship in the process.

At home, after Bill had gone to bed, Jane and Carter discussed the visit of Mr. Chase. "What do you think about the tutoring idea, darling?" asked Carter.

"You know I would be agreeable to anything that will help Bill. We can give it a try. We owe it to our son and to Mr. Chase, for his unusual interest in the matter."

"Well," commented Carter, "just between ourselves, we have not been totally ignorant of Bill's problems, but parents are not always quick, or willing, to face up to reality, and I guess we are no exception. Tomorrow we will go to New Exeter to see what we can do. We'll let Rosie pick Bill up at lunchtime. We can tell her we have business out of town. Bill is very fond of Rosie and I think he will be happy to have her come for him."

The next morning found the troubled parents in the office of the president of their alma mater. As much as they disliked to reveal that their son was not the excellent student that they had hoped he would be, they found that President Stanford listened sympathetically.

"I am glad you have come to us with your problem. It will be held in strictest confidence," said Dr. Stanford. "I believe we can help you. With your permission I will call the head of the Department of Elementary Education, Professor Clark."

Receiving the nod of approval, Dr. Stanford picked up his desk telephone and dialed. "Yes, Mary. Is Professor Clark in?"

"Yes, Dr. Stanford. Do you wish to speak with him?" said the voice on the phone.

"If you please!"

Professor Clark was soon on the phone. "Yes, Dr. Stanford."

"I have two people in my office whom I would like you to meet. Can you come in?"

"Yes, I'll be right over."

When the young man entered, President Stanford made the appropriate introductions, not omitting the fact that Jane and Carter were both alumni, that Jane had been the head librarian at one time at the college, and that Carter was now president of the Wellington City National Bank. Both President Stanford and Professor Clark exhibited a high regard for the recommendations of Superintendent Chase. Professor Clark requested his secretary to bring the card file of spring graduates in education who had not as yet secured teaching positions.

He pulled a 3x5 card from the hinged file. "Mabel King" it read, "Age: 22. Scholastic standing: Straight A."

"Here is a young lady I believe would make a good tutor. It seems that although several schools have sought her services, the right position has not been found. I remember Miss King being somewhat shy, having been reared on a tiny farm in the eastern Alleghenies. I rather imagine she wants something near her home, but since she hasn't found employment, she might be interested in coming to Wellington City. I also remember Miss King as being an excellent student, as indicated on her card here. I would be happy to contact her. If she is interested I could let you know and you folks could take it from there."

Carter responded, "Thank you, Professor Clark. Would you do that?"

A few days later Professor Clark called Carter at the bank and indicated that Miss King was very much interested in the position and that she was writing the Wellingtons. When Miss King's letter arrived, Jane opened it expectantly. It said, among other things, that she would come to their home for an interview at any time that was convenient for them. Jane, after consulting with Carter, replied immediately, arranging an interview.

Jane had asked Rosie to take William to a movie during the afternoon Miss King was to come for the interview. When she arrived, it was apparent that while the young lady was not given to aggressiveness, she was willing to answer all their questions.

"It's curious," said Carter, during the conversation, "that you are not already engaged in teaching. Is it that you don't care to leave home? You attended college for four years. Didn't you become accustomed to living away from home during that time?"

"Sir," the girl replied politely, "teaching positions are not as plentiful now as they once were, as you probably know. Also, most of the interviews involved schools a great distance from my home, too far, in fact to live at home. Besides the additional expense involved, I am much happier living with my family."

Carter reminded her that the position she was now considering entailed living at their home.

"I know, Mr. Wellington. I have become resigned to the fact that I don't have much choice but to take an assignment away from home."

Carter and Jane then described in detail their problem with Bill. Jane explained, "It seems he is unable to work in the presence of other children. Because of that fact, Superintendent Chase has suggested a tutor for what we hope will be only a short time. We would want you to remain here most of the time to observe Bill on a full-time basis. There is plenty of room here for you to have all the privacy you wish. Of course, we realize that you would want to return to your home for Christmas vacation and occasionally at other times throughout the year."

"The position is one I believe I would like," remarked Mabel, who had been accustomed to a much lower standard of living than was apparent in the Wellington home, "but before I decide definitely, I would like to meet your son."

"Very well," said Jane. "He and Rosie have gone out this afternoon, but they should be returning soon. Perhaps before you leave they will be here."

"There is one thing we haven't discussed—the matter of salary." Mabel was reluctant to broach the matter of remuneration.

"Since Mr. Chase has outlined the plan," said Carter, "I believe that he should be consulted as to the appropriate salary. I have no precedent to follow in respect to that matter. Also, I think the superintendent should have the opportunity to have a private interview with you. He will explain the arrangements he has in mind regarding your teaching status, as well as the financial consideration."

Carter then called Mr. Chase. "We have talked to Miss King at length and it appears that she will be very acceptable to us, if the position is acceptable to her. When do you wish to interview her?"

Mr. Chase requested that Miss King come to his office right away.

"Fine! I'll go right over. You will likely be hearing from Mr. Chase regarding my employment. Thank you very much, Mr. and Mrs. Wellington. It's been a pleasure talking to you. But I had hoped to meet Bill."

Just then the sound of the door opening, accompanied by voices, reached their ears. "Oh, here are Bill and Rosie now," reported Jane. Without revealing the purpose of Miss King's visit, Jane made the introductions.

"Hello, Bill," greeted Mabel. "How are you?"

"Okay," the noncommittal Bill said.

"Where have you been?"

"To the movies," answered Bill.

"Did you have a good time?"

Bill nodded his head in the affirmative.

"How old are you, Bill?"

Bill held up his right hand with his fingers spread apart, and the forefinger on the left hand.

"Six years old! I have a brother who is only seven. Next year you will be seven, too!"

So went Mabel's attempts to become acquainted with Bill. She then bid the Wellingtons good-bye and expressed her hope that she would be seeing them again.

After Miss King's departure, Jane and Carter were discussing the interview. They both agreed that her shyness would be overcome as she became more involved in the business and professional world. After college she had returned to the farm, where there was little opportunity for social life. But yet, how much opportunity would she have for socializing when almost every hour of the day would be spent tutoring a young child?

In the private interview with Miss King, Superintendent Chase revealed the entire story of William Carter Wellington— an only son of older, wealthy parents who was well-developed physically, showing no visible signs of mental retardation. The child's low I.Q. was obvious, but he was believed trainable, within limits, to read, write, and perhaps to handle simple figures. The superintendent explained the plan to award her an honorary teacher's position in the school system, with a commensurate salary to be borne by the Wellingtons.

"Do you think you can handle the position, Miss King? Did you meet the child?"

"Yes, I met Bill briefly in his home. He seems very shy, but I think I can help him. At least, I would like to try."

"When do you think you could begin teaching, Miss King?"

"I could begin as soon as you say."

"Well, today is Thursday. Could you be ready to start Monday of next week? You will need a few days to return to your home and make preparations. As you know, school regulations are that a child be in school attendance, or its equivalent, every day, unless he is ill. At the moment, young William is not in school, which is sad. He should not be losing these precious days."

So it was that Mabel King, slight of build, well-mannered, took up her abode at the Wellington home. Mabel wished to be as unobtrusive in her new position as possible and to interrupt the Wellington routine as little as necessary. Being of a quiet temperament, this was not difficult for her. By the end of the first day, Mabel and Bill appeared to have known one another for years. Rosie served all their meals in the breakfast room, leaving Jane, Carter, and Grandfather Porter to dine as usual in the dining room. That is the way teacher and pupil preferred it.

A small room secluded from the rest of the house became the schoolroom. In the room were a school desk, a blackboard, a desk for Mabel, and all the teaching aids to be found in any schoolroom. The school hours were the same as those at the public school, as no teacher, or no pupil, could do their best work when fatigued.

Even though this was Mabel's first position, she seemed to be one who had had a great deal of experience, for she knew just how to obtain the confidence of the child. In a matter of a few days, Bill was showing that he possessed a greater potential than anyone ever thought he had. But he couldn't understand why he had been withdrawn from his school.

"Mamma," Bill said at bedtime one night, "why me don't go school like Jack and Jimmy? I like at school."

"Daddy and I think you can learn better at home. Miss Mabel thinks so, too. She loves you. I hope you love her, too."

"Yes, Mamma, me love Miss Mabel."

Even though he was Miss Mabel's charge for several hours each day, Bill did not forget who his parents were, nor did Jane and Carter forget him. After school hours were over, in good weather, Bill and Mabel often went for walks in the park. They fed the swans, or watched the birds, or Bill joined the other children in foot races and other athletic games. Although Bill's mental capacities might be questioned, his physical prowess had never been lacking. Often he was the winner in his athletic aspirations, which afforded him a great deal of pride in himself.

When Bill and Miss Mabel returned to the house after their late afternoon activities and had dined together, Bill would join his family for the evening, at which time Carter and Jane would read children's stories, or the three would participate in table games. Mabel would retire to her comfortable room on the second floor of the home and would not see the child again until they met for breakfast the following day. In this manner, teacher and pupil, parents and child enjoyed an excellent relationship.

Each week Superintendent Chase visited the "schoolroom" just as he occasionally did other schoolrooms, to observe Bill's progress. Each week he then reported to Jane and Carter the wonderful progress Bill was making.

"It's nothing short of a miracle," he said. "I really believe we should continue the arrangement for another year."

So it went for the first school term. Bill, while making some progress, was not nearly so far advanced as Superintendent Chase would have the parents believe. Jane and Carter, wishing to believe the best of their son, took Mr. Chase at his word and did not give voice to the questions that were on their mind, fearing a truthful reply.

During the summer vacation, Mabel returned to her home and Bill, Jane, and Carter once again resumed a normal family relationship, spending a few weeks at the seashore.

When schooltime again arrived, both Mabel and Bill were refreshed. Bill's report card then indicated that he was a second grader. While the child could count and was learning the shapes and sounds of some of the letters of the alphabet, he was still far short of the achievements of other children at this point and Miss Mabel knew this. She disliked seeing the parents deceived as they were, but she could truthfully report to them their son was making progress.

Each year, as Superintendent Chase proposed the continuance of the program, the Wellingtons protested the lengthy duration of the arrangement. Mr. Chase continued to assure them of its success, stressing the possibility of regression if the procedure was discontinued. The parents would then reluctantly accede, year after year, to continue the program for still another school term, since they admitted that they could detect some progress, thus assuring themselves that their son was not what could be termed mentally retarded, only a slow learner. Thus, the superintendent's assurance of Bill's definite progress, and his fears of changing the environment; their complete trust in Mabel who also, to a lesser degree, admitted progress and improvement; and their own hopes that the arrangement had been thus far a definite benefit were sufficient arguments to cause Jane and Carter to agree to the plan through eight years of elementary school.

Although Mabel knew that her pupil had not nearly completed the equivalent of an elementary education despite his progress, she felt that she had been as successful as any teacher could have been and even though she had received repeated commendations from the Wellingtons as well as from Superintendent Chase, her conscience troubled her at times for not being entirely truthful.

Upon completing the eighth grade, students in Wellington City, along with students throughout the state, were required to pass what was known as the State Elementary Examination in order to graduate. These examinations were given at various points throughout the state by the local school superintendent; the students' papers were then submitted to the State Department of Education for grading. Students prepared extensively for these tests. While a participant was permitted two opportunities each year, if necessary, to achieve a passing grade, some were unable to do so. Unless the child had reached the age where school attendance was no longer necessary, he was required to repeat the eighth grade year after year until a satisfactory examination paper had been submitted.

William Wellington was no exception to the regulation regarding the state examination. Superintendent Chase insisted the test be given to William in his schoolroom at the Wellington home in familiar surroundings. Present for the examination, in addition to William, would be Miss King and Superintendent Chase, whose responsibility it was to administer the examination to all students in Wellington City. The two older members of the threesome supplied the answers to questions that William did not know and William would then laboriously copy them on the examination sheets supplied by Superintendent Chase. This procedure was followed for each subject. No student had ever worked harder to present neat, acceptable examination papers! In many cases, it was necessary to rewrite a test several times before an acceptable paper could be submitted.

But pass the examination he did, at least to the satisfaction of Mr. Chase, and was issued a diploma which read:

> BE IT KNOWN that WILLIAM CARTER WELLINGTON has successfully completed all required courses and examinations for his graduation from the Elementary Schools of the Commonwealth of Pennsylvania.
>
> Signed: JOHN A. MONROE
> Superintendent of Public Instruction
> Commonwealth of Pennsylvania

Everyone concerned, Jane and Carter, Miss King, Superintendent Chase, and of course William himself, was extremely proud of the embellished document—so proud, in fact, that the document was framed and hung in the library of the Wellington home, next to similar documents issued long ago to Jane and Carter as well as to Grandfather and Grandmother Porter.

After eight years with William, Mabel was rewarded with a position in the school system which she held for many years. But she never quite absolved herself of the guilt she felt for her part in the deception, even though she had done her utmost for the boy. She often asked herself throughout the years, "What if *nothing* had been done for the child?"

8.

GRANT CHASE, AS SCHOOL superintendent, had been cognizant that the day would arrive when William Wellington, having been awarded his elementary school diploma, would be ready to enter high school, at least theoretically. Mr. Chase was also cognizant of the fact that the boy was not scholastically prepared to enter the city's public high school system.

During this same period, a time characterized by student unrest and lack of discipline generally, with a corresponding decline in esteem for the quality of public high school education, many of the more affluent families, who feared for the safety, habits, and morals of their offspring, revived the trend toward private boarding academies. While the trend was by no means an avalanche, a few of the wealthier families even in Wellington City had chosen to enroll their youth in these schools, feeling they would receive a better education and also be protected from the undesirable influences thought to be present in many public high schools.

The superintendent considered this trend toward private schools a possible solution to the question of the further education of young William Wellington. Among private boarding schools there existed a wide range of quality. Some were high-grade preparatory schools which far exceeded the quality of most public school systems. Some were coeducational, but the majority of these schools and academies limited their enrollment to one sex, more generally boys. In addition to the usual high school curriculum, a significant number offered military training and were known as military academies, although these had no official connection with the government. Some, especially the coeducational and girls' schools, stressed religious training of the students and were principally sponsored by church organizations. Others were merely "snob" schools, for the offspring of parents who wished to impress their peers or who were guilty of wishing to send their children away from home for a few months of the year to be free of parental responsibility.

Not generally well known was the fact that not all private schools were of the excellent quality ascribed to them. While most of these schools were nonprofit institutions, generally of high caliber, others were strictly operated as profitable business ventures for their owners. Even among the latter type some were of good quality, but generally their appeal was to the wealthy who had experienced the misfortune of becoming the parents of children having behavioral and learning problems. Many such schools were emphasizing strong athletic or military programs to compensate somewhat for the students' academic deficiencies. A parent, observing a son wearing a uniform of a captain or starring in an exciting basketball game or other sports event, could not be other than proud, and often would overlook his educational shortcomings.

J. Carter Wellington, being an informed man, was well aware of the potential of some of the private academies and had at least given some thought to their possible advantage over public schools for William, now that he had graduated from elementary school. But as president of the local school board, he was fearful of public reaction to the chief elective officer of a public high school sending his own son to a private academy.

Meanwhile, Mr. Chase, without consulting the Wellingtons and in the interest of avoiding trouble by William entering Wellington City High School, had located, after much investigation, a school which he felt would serve William Wellington's needs, namely, New London Military Academy. This school in previous years had enjoyed a good reputation by emphasizing scholastic training of boys as well as offering a vigorous military and physical fitness program. More recently, the school had fallen into the hands of questionable private ownership, which was exploiting its previous reputation in order to achieve a handsome profit for its owners.

The school was catering to wealthy, doting parents whose sons, although somewhat lacking in scholastic prowess, generally were not lacking in their physical capabilities. For this reason, the school's athletic program still possessed the high qualities that were missing in its scholastic standards, although, officially, the institution still met all the standards required by the state to continue in operation. Actually, the venture was an attempt to offer a program adapted to each student's academic abilities, while at the same time reporting to the parents, whether a fact or not, the excellent progress of their son or sons. However, its principal stress was on its physical and military program.

The school's ambitious recruiting program included a bonus to any public school official who was able to influence the enrollment of a student. Thus, Mr. Chase, in addition to filling the needs of Bill Wellington could expect to reap a few dollars in the transaction. The task was to sell the idea to the Wellingtons, a task which he undertook with great fervor.

Superintendent Chase approached the Wellingtons in their home one evening shortly after their son's graduation to discuss the boy's future. He began, "Mr. and Mrs. Wellington, congratulations! Your son has graduated from the first step in his education. What future plans do you have for the lad?"

"Well," replied Carter, "Jane and I have always expected that Bill would be enrolled in the public high school here in Wellington City. Don't you think he can handle the curriculum?"

"Perhaps, but have you ever thought of a boarding school?"

"A boarding school?" Jane and Carter echoed in unison.

"Yes, we have many good private schools within a short travelling distance, where you would be able to visit him often and Bill could also return home frequently. Perhaps being away from home for a while would be good for the boy. I have in mind a school where he would associate with his social and economic peers rather than with the rough, unruly students often encountered in a public high school.

"Mr. Wellington, as school board president, you are surely familiar with what I mean. I have been doing some investigating and have located a good school less than forty miles away that comes highly recommended by some very well-informed sources in the field of private education. I refer to New London Military Academy."

Mr. Chase continued, "Military schools, generally speaking,

are highly selective in the acceptance of their students. Following these recommendations, I visited the academy myself without mentioning the reason and was most favorably impressed with all phases of its operation—the curriculum, the physical plant, and the personnel. I am sure I can arrange a tour for you, Jane, and William and, if you desire, I will be happy to accompany you."

"This is so very thoughtful of you, Mr. Chase," responded Jane. "You are in a good position to know about these schools. Your description of New London Academy interests me, as I am sure it does my husband. Carter, what do you think?

"Well, Mr. Chase, we'll talk the matter over and let you know in a few days."

"Very well, Mr. Wellington. I will wait to hear from you, but I do hope you will give New London serious consideration."

Mr. Chase departed very satisfied with himself that the groundwork had been laid to enroll young William Carter Wellington in the New London Military Academy.

That same evening Mr. Chase called the headmaster at New London Military Academy, Mr. Vandermere, and revealed to him that he had a prospective student whose affluent parents were anxious that their son be enrolled in a good school. Mr. Chase apprised Mr. Vandermere of the entire situation and they both knew that the Wellingtons would find it difficult to enroll their scholastically deficient son in any school except one that specialized in the type of education such as this one provided. Of course, the Wellingtons suspected it too, but were too proud to admit the fact.

After Mr. Chase's departure, a serious discussion began between Jane and Carter Wellington. Jane spoke first. "I wonder why Mr. Chase is so interested that Bill be enrolled in New London. Doesn't he think we are knowledgeable enough to select the school we wish our son to attend? Does he have a financial or other special interest in the school? He didn't tell us how many students the school has. I have never heard of the school, have you?"

"Yes," replied Carter. "I have heard of the school, but I am not sure of the quality. I would like to do some investigating myself. What do you think about going away to school, Bill?"

Bill was reluctant to show much interest, but being the obedient, agreeable child that he was, he said, "It would be okay. Would you visit me much? Could I take my guppies?"

"Of course, darling, we would visit you often, and you could come home often, too," encouraged Jane. "I am sure you could take your guppies."

Later, after Bill had retired, Carter observed to Jane, "While we may not appreciate that Mr. Chase is encouraging us to enroll Bill in New London, the fact of the matter is, between you and me, our son is not a top-notch student, and any school willing to enroll him as a regular student would be less than the best. Yet what choice do we have?" Even though Carter and Jane had realized for some years that it would be questionable whether or not their son could cope with the normal high school program, that night was the first time either of them had expressed any doubt concerning the matter.

The necessary arrangements were made with Superintendent Chase to visit the New London campus the following week. The forty-mile journey was punctuated with conversation between the adults, with little contribution from Bill. As Mr. Chase stopped the car at the main gate of the campus, a uniformed guard waved them on. Apparently, while the car was moving slowly up the driveway to the Administration Building, the guard had communicated their arrival on the intercom system, since the doorman was ready to open the door as they approached. The doorman then assisted Jane and William as they alighted from the car and the four members of the party entered the building. Inside, Mr. Vandermere was waiting while two uniformed assistants stood by at attention. After the proper introductions were made, Mr. Vandermere began, "We have a wonderful school here, as I am sure you will agree after you have seen the premises. My assistants here will show you the complete plant. Please feel free to ask them any questions you wish."

The procession then began, with the two assistants, Mr. Justice and Mr. Morgan, leading the way, followed by Jane and Carter, with Bill and Mr. Chase walking together at the rear. Mr. Justice was quick to emphasize the exclusive qualities of the school. "Mr. and Mrs. Wellington, you can be assured that we are selective in choosing our student body. As you probably already know, only boys from well-bred homes and with high scholastic standings are admitted to this institution. Some come from as far away as New York City, where the supply of good schools is unlimited, yet these boys, or perhaps their parents, choose this school, rather than one in their own city. Let me emphasize, particularly, our fine athletic program, as we understand your son is athletically inclined."

So the procession continued through all the facilities of the campus, including the classrooms, dormitories, dining room, swimming pool, recreational facilities, chapel, auditorium, gymnasium, and the park like grounds. Nothing was omitted that would be a selling point for the school. William was excited about it all, too, and insofar as he was able to express himself, let it be known that he was eager about the prospects of attending such an institution. Mr. Justice and Mr. Morgan were almost assured before the tour was completed that New London Military Academy had a new recruit.

Returning to Headmaster Vandermere's office, Jane and Carter were pressed for their opinion of the school.

"Of course," Mr. Vandermere began, "There are no students here now since it is summer vacation, but I believe you must agree that we have a fine physical plant here, do we not? Not only that which you can see is of the finest quality, but we believe the academic qualities cannot be matched."

"Yes, you do have a very fine appearing school, sir," Carter commented, "but I dislike being too hasty in making a decision. This is the first school we have visited and we would like to delay any decision for a while. After all, young William has just received his diploma from elementary school and we haven't had time to decide about his further education."

"Mr. Wellington," replied the headmaster, "Mr. Chase assures me your son would have no difficulty academically, or with the physical or military program. We are willing to accept your son upon the recommendation of Superintendent Chase. Why don't we complete the paperwork today?" Mr. Vandermere was already beginning to execute the necessary forms.

"No! I am a businessman too, and I wish to dwell on the matter for a few days."

When the Wellingtons were again at home, Jane began the

conversation, "I wonder why Mr. Vandermere was so anxious that we sign the application today. Do you think there is something about the transaction he doesn't want us to know?"

"Perhaps he is afraid we might decide to send Bill elsewhere, and he wants our name on the dotted line before we have the opportunity to think about it and decide against the school. He knows the psychology of a successful salesman. Even though I have almost decided to enroll William in New London, I don't want to appear too anxious."

A few weeks later young William Wellington, and his guppies, had been formally accepted at New London Military Academy. As expected, the boy adapted well to the athletic and military features of the school. As the weeks passed he demonstrated his excellent coordination as an athlete in the sports program. Glowing reports came from the school to the parents covering all aspects of his school work, including his scholastic progress, even though his achievements in the latter left much to be desired.

Although freshmen were not members of the intervarsity athletic teams, they were permitted to train with the upperclassmen in anticipation of participating on these teams in succeeding years. The second week of school, during football training, William showed sufficient ability to receive assurance from the coach that, with diligent practice he could become a member of the team. But it was not until the beginning of the basketball season that William showed the most promise. While still a freshman, his performance was so outstanding that, contrary to regulations, he actually was allowed to participate in some regular intervarsity games.

William also adapted well to the military training program. In fact, his general enthusiasm was such that even his scholastic aptitude demonstrated much improvement also. The closely guarded records indicated at the year's end that his academic grades had improved to the sixth-grade level—a full grade above that which tests indicated he possessed at the time he entered the school.

Not only did William enjoy and show marked superiority in sports, he also enjoyed the other students. On occasion he had asked and received permission for friends to accompany him on

71

his weekend visits to his home. The new life was, to him, quite different than that which he had known at home in past years.

Bill's sophomore year was even more exciting. Although he was not yet a regular on the football team, his performance strongly suggested that the following year he would be a team member. But what thrilled both him and his parents most was his performance in basketball. Not only did he make the regular team as a guard, he was the second highest scorer for the team. Meanwhile, slow but steady improvement was noted in his scholastic record and in his military training his performance was more than adequate.

During his third year he continued to show steady improvement over the prior year. In football, he was used from time to time as a lineman and participated in some spectacular games. Still, it was basketball in which William continued to demonstrate unusual skill. He was moved from guard to center and as such attained the highest scoring record of the team; it was, in fact, the highest scoring record in the history of the school's basketball program. In the military program he was advanced to lieutenant. Even his academic record continued to improve, although slowly. Except for his notable athletic record as encouragement he perhaps would have made little or no academic advance, but his enthusiasm for the school forced him into exerting his best efforts which, no doubt, accounted for his achievements in this direction.

Bill's senior year was his banner year! While he showed improvement in the other sports, his performance in basketball continued to be characterized by outstanding success. Elected captain of the team and playing center position, his brilliant performance and the cooperation of his supporting team members had placed New London Academy in the final game of the private league annual championship, after having beaten many teams from the larger, more formidable, schools.

Playing on New London's floor, in a contest with Greenville Academy, the score stood at 80 to 81 in favor of the visiting team. The crowd was in a frenzy! Then, miraculously recovering the ball from the opposition, Bill executed a long shot. After rimming the basket for what seemed an interminable period of time, the ball sank into the basket, winning for New London its first championship under the new management. Its fans, wild with excitement, jumped to their feet, and, clapping their hands, shouted, "Hooray for Wellington! We want Wellington!" Bill was carried off the floor, his two arms raised, on the shoulders of two of his fellow team members. But no one in the crowd was more excited than Bill's parents. They were invited to an After-the-Game party honoring all the team members, but most especially, the one who had delivered the game for his school. The entire episode converted Jane and Carter from what would be called a passing interest in the game to avid fans.

This first championship victory under the school's new management did much to establish its reputation as one deserving an important place in sports competition. Mr. Vandermere's only regret was that Bill was a senior and would be unable to repeat the performance in future years, but his interest in Bill and his progress was such that he called him to his office for a series of examinations which Superintendent Chase had supplied. The examination papers were then secretly submitted, under an assumed name, by Mr. Chase to the Department of Education of the Commonwealth of Pennsylvania.

Mr. Vandermere's satisfaction that an academically retarded youth had actually passed the State Elementary Examination, unaided, surpassed all of Bill's other achievements. At least three years of scholastic advancement were attained while Bill had been a student at the school, an achievement not to be taken lightly.

Finally came the day of graduation, when the students, in their black caps and gowns, marched down the aisle of the school auditorium to the platform. How proud each parent was, but none more so than two certain parents from Wellington City. Their emotions could scarcely be contained. Tears of happiness welled up in Jane's eyes; the expression of happiness written in Carter's face, as he gazed upon that one special boy awaiting his diploma, had not been equaled since that day some eighteen years earlier when he had first gazed upon the child Jane presented him.

William's graduation had brought happiness to others also: to

Mr. Vandermere, who was proud not only because of William's progress, but also because he had succeeded in graduating another wealthy student, thus assuring the present as well as, no doubt, the future financial status of the school; to Mr. Chase, because he had averted what could have been an embarrassing situation for him; and, of course, to William himself who, in addition to graduating from high school, had now pleasantly experienced living away from home and had grown up in the process.

9.

THE APPLICATION OF WILLIAM Carter Wellington was among others received for admission to the fall term of New Exeter College. William's application indicated he had graduated from the Wellington City elementary schools, that he was an alumnus of the New London Military Academy with a high scholastic standing, that he had participated in athletic programs and other extracurricular activities. A diploma, as evidence of graduation from a secondary school, was required for admission in New Exeter and the members of the admitting staff were unfamiliar with the recent problems of New London Military Academy some eighty miles away.

Young Wellington's application also indicated that his forebears were graduates of New Exeter and members of its supporting denomination. William's mother, the former Jane Porter, was recalled by some of the older members of the staff as having been head librarian at the school, before her marriage to William's father. The name Wellington was well-known at the school, not only for the contribution of its members to the area as business entrepreneurs, but for their coveted financial position. With such a background, the processing of William's application was a mere formality.

With the beginning of the fall term, William entered the freshman class eager to pursue his further education. His parents, too, were eager for their only child to finish his formal education and to take his place in the business community as a successor to his father and grandfather as president of the local bank. The fact that William's intellectual capacities were not what would be termed "normal" was not immediately apparent; if any of his instructors suspected him to be lacking in this area, it was blamed on the process of adjustment to college life.

75

Even though William's mental deficiencies went unnoticed in the beginning, there was no mistake on this point after a period of evaluation of each student by the instructors. It was evident that this student, the son of a famous family in which such a phenomenon would be least expected, was considerably lacking in intellectual aptitude. "How did he ever reach college level of academic training?" they asked themselves and one another.

In spite of William's parents' guidance in the selection of a business administration course as preparation for his future as a banker, the young man found it difficult, even impossible, to comprehend the course of study. By the time a month of classroom work and study had passed, it was recognized that William did not belong in college. At a faculty meeting, a month after school had begun, it was recommended that the student be dismissed for failing to meet academic standards of the school.

New Exeter College, the traditional citadel of advanced learning for Methodism in western Pennsylvania, including the Wellington City community and especially those whose roots were embedded in the Methodist church of that city, had come upon difficult times. Lester P. Green, its new president, had been given full power by its trustees to do whatever was necessary to maintain the school's accreditation, which was severely threatened.

The college was founded by the Methodist church in the early years of the nineteenth century as a training school for the clergy of the denomination. As the years passed, the curriculum of the school was broadened to include teacher training courses and was duly accredited by the state; and near the end of the century it had been expanded sufficiently to be fully accredited by both the state and the regional associations as a liberal arts college, granting both liberal arts and science degrees. Although widely recognized as a school of high quality, its enrollment was never large, with fewer than one thousand students, most of whom lived in the surrounding areas. Such established families as the Wellingtons and the Porters were counted among its graduates who contributed significantly to its support, as did many other members of the Wellington City Methodist Church.

76

Early in the twentieth century, in order to improve the quality of education, greater demands upon colleges to upgrade their staff began to be made by the regional accrediting agency. Demands were also made to even further expand the curriculum and to overhaul the physical plants and equipment. Also, since many new colleges were being founded, New Exeter wished to be competitive. Yet the school was in a precarious position, for dwindling support, due to a general deterioration in the economic circumstances of the area, and a declining population had resulted in fewer endowments and enrollments.

Finally, the Middle States Association warned member institutions, including New Exeter, to meet its demands or lose their membership in the Association. As was the case with many of the older colleges in the country, New Exeter's buildings had seen better days. Thus the college was facing twin tragedies: dwindling support and loss of accreditation.

At last the Middle States Association issued the final ultimatum to New Exeter: update the library within three years or face disaccreditation. An emergency meeting of the trustees was called by President Stanford and the formal notice read:

Dr. Harry S. Stanford, President
New Exeter College

You are hereby advised that unless the library facilities of New Exeter College are improved to the satisfaction of this Association within the space of three years from the date of this notice, accreditation will be withdrawn.

Accompanying the notice was a list of specifications which must be incorporated into an approved library.

Dr. Stanford, addressing the assembled board, stated in firm tones, "Gentlemen, I do not need to tell you that this school does not have the funds to meet the demands of the Middle States Association. To bring the library into compliance would mean the replacing of the present building, stocking it with many hundreds of books and other types of literature, and staffing it with additional qualified personnel." Dr. Stanford then enumerated the list of demands supplied with the notice.

"You are totally aware," he said, "that under present circumstances these things are impossible. Do any of you gentlemen have a solution to the predicament? Of course, we have all known for quite some time that New Exeter was not, to put it mildly, in a coveted state of affairs, but we had hoped that circumstances somehow would change for the better, and the day of reckoning could be postponed."

Low groans and murmurings could be heard from each of the eight men who heard the reading of the notice and the comments of Dr. Stanford. After a few minutes, but what seemed an eternity, one member rose to speak. "Mr. President, as we have just been reminded, this order comes to us as no surprise, but our hands have been tied. Now we must come to a decision. I move that another meeting of this board be held with the governing board of the supporting denomination one week from now."

So it was agreed. The meeting was adjourned on this sad note, with no real hope that the situation could be remedied.

Much discussion took place at the next meeting, but no real solutions were forthcoming. It was suggested that the college merge with another Methodist college facing similar problems, but the idea was ruled out as impractical. Late in the session Dr. Stanford stood bravely behind the podium and spoke.

"Gentlemen, perhaps the school needs a change of administration. I have served many years in my present capacity. It has been my aim to serve the school well, but I believe it is time for a change, both for the school and for me. I hereby submit my resignation as president of New Exeter College, effective at the end of the present term. Thank you!" He then left the podium and sat down.

Murmurs of surprise could be heard among those present. The chairman of the representatives from the church then took the podium. He spoke, "Sirs, this is a surprise to me as I know it is to many of you. Dr. Stanford has served us for a long, long time and has been a definite asset to this school. He has spent many years in its behalf—some of them agonizing years. It was Dr. Stanford's able leadership that brought the school to a place of recognition, a place where the youth of this area could obtain a quality education, and many of our leading citizens have gained much because of this devotion to his task. It is not through any dereliction of duty on his part that the school finds itself in its present difficulty, and I pray that Dr. Stanford does not feel that it is. However, I feel that we have no alternative but to accept his resignation. I thank you!"

A member of the Methodist group moved that the resignation be accepted. Another member seconded the motion. Thus it was that the school would shortly be without a president. One of the newer members of the board must have been waiting for just such a moment. He had a plan formulated to save the college. He proposed to appoint as president a man who, in addition to his qualifications as an educator, also possessed qualities as a professional fund raiser with a proven record of success in this area. The author of the proposal was a less conservative gentleman who was more abreast of the times as far as the operation of small denominational colleges was concerned. He further proposed, "Of course, this board would find it necessary to allow such a person free rein to pursue whatever course of action he deems necessary to achieve results, and to compensate the gentleman accordingly."

Whatever objections the denominational leaders had against the unorthodox proposal, and there were many, they were not of sufficient strength to kill the proposal, since there was little choice of action if the college were to survive. Consequently, the proposal received a favorable vote. The next step was to locate the man they were looking for, and the initiator of the proposal was the man delegated the task, which wouldn't be easy.

After a long search the man for the job of delivering New Exeter from the abyss of oblivion was found—one who had saved other institutions facing similar difficulties, one whose methods would be considered extremely questionable, one who knew how to take advantage of human vanity. Orthodox or unorthodox, questionable or otherwise, honest or not, Lester P. Green was the man who could obtain what New Exeter needed and needed then—money.

When the newly appointed president was confronted with the recommendation for William's dismissal, he requested that the young man be brought to his office, according to his established policy.

"William," President Green began, "some of our students are

being given special scholastic tests to determine at what level they should be placed. Perhaps you are not working up to your potential. These tests will tell us whether or not you are enrolled in classes at your proper level of advancement."

"Yes, sir," the polite William replied, believing President Green was sincere in that which he implied. "I will be happy to take the tests."

William then was examined on various levels of mathematics, reading ability, composition, and penmanship, as well as oral expression. The final result was assessed as a slightly mentally retarded student, especially as far as advanced learning was concerned, but one who appeared perfectly normal to casual social contacts. Now to be decided was what course of action to follow. Under most circumstances, the student would be dismissed forthright, but President Green foresaw a potential benefit to be gained by retaining this young man in the college.

Although President Green was new to the area, he had had enough time to search out those citizens who could be a definite asset to his plan for the school and for himself as its administrator. During this search, Mr. Green had made himself acquainted with William's background: the only son of a wealthy family and heir apparent to two of the largest fortunes in the area; the parents and grandparents important figures in the founding and support of the Methodist church of Wellington City, the college, and even Wellington City itself; forebears who for several generations had been successful as owners of the largest bank of Wellington City and, indeed, of the area. All these factors added up to a giant total in the eyes of Mr. Green. This student was too important to dismiss!

The new president lost no time in outlining a plan to further William's education. After William returned to his classes, a letter to J. Carter and Jane Wellington was quickly placed in the mail:

Dear Mr. and Mrs. Wellington,

It is requested that you meet with me at your earliest convenience for a conference concerning your son William. Any time within the next day or two will be satisfactory.

The missive was the source of considerable uneasiness in the

Wellington household. Nevertheless, without further communication, Jane and Carter travelled to New Exeter. After the usual formal greetings were exchanged, President Green began, "I am somewhat hesitant to inform you that your son is experiencing some difficulty in school. It appears that it might be well, or even necessary, to give him special help. We here at the school are aware that you no doubt consider a college degree very important to William, and I don't mean to convey that he will not be able to obtain that degree with the proper guidance."

Carter and Jane remained silent as President Green continued. "Uh . . . ," as he searched for the words that would produce the results he wished, "I understand that you, Mrs. Wellington, were once the chief librarian here. More than likely, at that time the library met all the standards. But times have changed, and the facilities have deteriorated, and now New Exeter has been requested by the Middle States Association to replace its library or lose its accreditation. A few months ago we were given three years to remedy that situation. New libraries are not easy to come by, as you know. New Exeter does not have the funds to meet the demands of the Middle States Association. Would you be willing to – uh – contribute a substantial portion–uh–even the major portion–of the funds needed for construction of a new library?"

President Green had finally been able to ask, in unmistakable terms, just the question he wanted to ask. Yet he had not finished.

"The library fund, as it now stands, is almost nonexistent. When I say 'the major portion,' I mean to indicate that a contributor must be in a position to underwrite virtually the entire cost. Of course, the facility could, if you wish, be named in your honor."

Carter and Jane were stunned, to say the least. "Are you inferring, President Green, that unless we agree to finance a new library it will be impossible for our son to graduate?" voiced Carter.

"No, not necessarily, but his graduation would be placed in a different perspective. You are both alumni of this institution and I know you would be proud to honor your alma mater by such a gesture. It would demonstrate your faith in the college, the college that would serve future generations. I will make it my personal responsibility to give William all the help he needs to bring his achievements up to the standards of the school and to see that he is among those participating in the graduation exercises four years from now."

At the sight of tears forming in Jane's eyes, Carter, although deeply moved but able to control his emotions, consoled his wife by tenderly caressing her about the shoulders. He thoroughly understood what the president was saying. If their fondest hopes were not to be dashed—the hope of their only son continuing in the family tradition—he could not refuse the request. Carter's eyes met Jane's and in them he could read her agreement with what he knew they had to do.

So the agreement for the exchange was made. New Exeter would get a new library and William Wellington would receive a college degree.

"One more request I must make of you, Mr. and Mrs. Wellington. Of course, you realize," President Green warned, "the details of this transaction must remain a private matter between us."

"Of course," echoed Carter. But would, or could, the transaction remain a private matter?

President Green's plan to assure William of a degree was to assign a private tutor to William. Each faculty member was then pledged to issue to William the minimum passing grade in all subjects, regardless of his performance. The dedicated staff members were astounded at such a request, some even to the point of resigning. But after consideration of the drastic consequences President Green threatened to impose: loss of benefits, refusal of recommendations to other schools, and so on, they steeled themselves against the atrocity and obeyed his instructions.

The construction of the new library was, indeed, a beautiful sight to behold and the attendant noises of hammer, saw, and construction machinery were music to the ears of President Green. One of the terms of the agreement was about to be fulfilled.

The fulfillment of the remaining portion of the agreement was also in sight. Young William's tutor had been well-picked.

Limited as they were, William's achievements, under the tutelage of Professor Henessey, developed to an unexpected level. To attain such results, the professor had spent long, patient hours, but he had been given the challenge and he vowed to meet it. Even though he had misgivings as to why President Green had deemed that the graduation of his charge was so important, his dedication was undiminished.

In William's senior year, President Green conducted an extended examination of the boy, in his office. Without aid, the young man completed the tests.

The results indicated an educational level equivalent to midway through the junior year of a standard high school course. Only President Green knew that William had been given the examination and the results were never revealed.

So it was that William Carter Wellington was among the new alumni of New Exeter College and President Lester P. Green accomplished that which had been expected of him.

One event was to mar the sense of elation and happiness at William's graduation and entry into the business world. His grandfather Porter was denied the joy of witnessing these important achievements of his only grandson. The elderly patriarch had passed away quietly only a few days before, but he had lived long enough to be proud that his namesake would be carrying on the integrity of his family.

10.

*I*T WAS WITH MUCH JOY and anticipation that Carter and Jane Wellington journeyed to New Exeter during the afternoon of the day preceding the graduation exercises.

"Carter," said Jane excitedly, "I just can't remember when I have been as happy as I am today, unless it was the day you proposed to me, or our wedding, or the discovery that we were to become parents, or William's birth. Even the happiness we experienced upon his graduation from New London does not compare to the event we are about to celebrate."

Jane had listed some of the happy events which had taken place in her life, not necessarily, however, in the order of elation which those events had brought to her. If she had been requested to name those events in their order of importance, she would have, indeed, been at a loss to do so. Jane continued, "It all seems too good to be true. Now, after twenty-two years of sometimes joy and sometimes doubt and sadness, we are experiencing the culmination of all our efforts and hopes, which seems too good to be true."

"Yes," responded Carter. "I, too, have been asking myself, 'Can it really be true that William is graduating from college?' Often my feelings over the years have fluctuated between doubt and hope."

After the pair had been comfortably settled in the most elaborate of the college guest rooms which had been arranged for their overnight stay, they walked across the parkway to view once again the magnificent new library which had been named in their honor. Carter and Jane had first visited the site at the ground-breaking ceremonies more than two years before. They first visited the completed building at the dedication a year later. It was then they witnessed the prominent letters "T–H–E

W-E-L-L-I-N-G-T-O-N L-I-B-R-A-R-Y" molded into the concrete above the main entrance. Several months prior to the dedication they had been present at the laying of the cornerstone. In addition to the usual items placed in the cornerstone of any such building—a copy of local newspapers of the day, a Bible, and other memorabilia—Carter and Jane were pleased to know that a copy of the contract for the original library, which contained the signatures of its Board of Trustees, including those of their paternal grandfathers, Thomas Wellington and Franklin Porter, had been removed from the cornerstone of the former building at the time of its demolition and was placed in the cornerstone of the new library, along with a copy of the contract for its construction.

What a feeling of pride it gave the pair as they walked through the beautifully landscaped grounds where the newly planted trees, as well as the mature ones which remained on the grounds of the old building, were clothed in fresh new leaves of spring, and where gardeners were even then busy planting seedlings in well-prepared earth, in anticipation of the colorful blooms that would further enhance the beauty of the surroundings.

Carter and Jane entered the building through the double swinging doors into the foyer and then into the main room. All about them were shelves, well-filled with not only the most modern reference books, but with many other types of literature, new and old. The second floor, reached by a wide curving stairway, was equally well-stocked, all arranged in the most convenient manner for easy access by those who would use the facility. In addition to the librarians' desks, both floors were supplied with an adequate number of reading tables surrounded by comfortable chairs. The entire scene brought back memories to Jane of the days when, in the old library, she had served her alma mater. Brought back to reality, Jane walked with her husband back to Stanley Hall and to the well-appointed room where they would spend the night.

Proud as they were of the new library and the fact that it was possible for them to make such a contribution to the institution which had meant so much to them, they still felt mixed emotions about the circumstances under which it had been built. Even though they were full of gratitude for the interest shown to their son, they realized that the school had had ulterior motives in seeing William complete his education.

President and Mrs. Green had extended an invitation to Jane and Carter to dine with them in their home in the evening. At the small private dinner which included only the two couples, conversation was both animated and patronizing. President Green revealed his doubts during the first weeks of school that their son would be able to master a college-level program but, he continued, "After I, myself, had administered thorough tests, I was convinced that the potential for success was present. Despite apparently diligent efforts of earlier teachers, it appeared that William had been inadequately prepared. I felt that the handicap could be overcome by concentrated effort and that at the same time he would be able to pursue his current studies."

President Green related his satisfaction that after four years of dedication, not only by the members of the faculty, but by the school administration itself and, most importantly, by William and his parents, their efforts had been well rewarded.

"To be sure," President Green continued, "your son is not and never will be a genius, but he has been able to meet the acceptable standards of the school, which, in itself, is to the young man's credit. There is no doubt but that William will be able to compete in the business world fully equal to a majority of his peers. Do you realize that only a small portion of the population, generally, has graduated from college? I am confident that with some orientation, your son will be capable of taking his place as a worthy successor to his father and other forebears."

Jane and Carter were pleased to hear all that President Green had to say, yet their acceptance of his words was not without reservation. Could it be said that his statements were without a degree of credibility or truthfulness?

The Wellingtons returned to their room after the dinner in a cheerful spirit.

"Jane, my dear," said Carter, as he tenderly embraced his wife, "the long, hard battle is over and victory is at hand. It has been with much effort and anxiety that we have reached this point. Without the teamwork we have both put into Bill's education, as well as the help of his teachers throughout the years, we would never be in this room upon this occasion. It has taken almost a quarter of a century to develop the story thus far, and it is not yet finished. True, Bill is graduating and is about to enter the business world, but what lies ahead for him, for us? Of course, none of us know what the future has in store, but our situation, if not unique, is rare. We have told ourselves that Bill would take his place in the bank following the footsteps of his father, grandfather, and many generations back. Were all our expectations and hopes merely wishful thinking?"

Jane responded as she gently stroked Carter's thinning and greying hair, "I know, Carter, I have always had those same feelings. I have never quite accepted the idea that Bill was not a normal child. Yet, if we had not accepted the obvious, where would he be today? Would he have been able even to complete elementary school? It has been worth all the effort we have put into the project and even more. Don't you agree?"

"Certainly, dear. Under the circumstances we wouldn't have wanted it any other way, would we?"

These exchanges of communication were only indications of some of their innermost feelings that Carter and Jane put into words that evening, the evening to which both had looked forward to for many years.

A businessman as alert and as successful as Carter Wellington is not easy to deceive. Acknowledging the fact that his son was not the usual child early in the boy's childhood, he had accepted the various assurances and programs proposed to him for William's education in the faint hope that Bill would not be a failure in life, just as a dying man accepts radical surgery, because there is no alternative available. Now this undying faith was being rewarded.

Jane and Carter each had silently borne their misgivings because neither wished to inflict emotional pain upon the other. Yet Jane had refrained from revealing that she, perhaps to a greater extent than Carter, if such be possible, believed in ultimate victory.

The baring of their souls to one another removed a heavy burden from each, bringing about a feeling of light heartedness neither had felt for many years. They felt like new persons. As they peered through the window at the new library and grounds, now with its brilliant floodlights even more enhancing its beauty, both agreed the cost, even though tremendous in dollars and cents, was the best investment they had ever made.

The next day, as the name "William Carter Wellington" was called, a handsome young man in black cap and gown stepped out to receive the customary handshake and the long-awaited diploma signifying that the recipient had completed the required courses to qualify for a Bachelor of Science degree in business administration. No parents were ever more proud of any son or daughter than those of Bill Wellington.

As the three returned to Wellington City that beautiful spring Sunday afternoon, the spirits of both parents and son soared. They talked about their plans for the next few weeks. Although William was anxious to begin work at the bank, each member of the family looked ahead to a vacation, a very special vacation, to celebrate William's graduation. Even though the family made a journey to a seaside resort each summer, or to some other equally relaxing spot, Carter and Jane wanted this vacation to be something different. They had given much thought to this holiday. What, or where should it be? Finally, at Carter's suggestion, it was decided that their honeymoon trip would be repeated with certain variations. They could again relive those happy days when, as newlyweds, Carter and Jane had visited that part of the world. William had never taken such a trip and the anticipation of an ocean voyage excited him.

Carter and Jane had made all the arrangements. They would take the train to New York, just as Carter and Jane had done many years earlier. From the nation's largest city they would embark on one of the most luxurious liners ever to float. A few days later the vessel would arrive in the Caribbean tropics where they would enjoy disembarking at the various ports of call, where they would be able to taste of another culture, where the people would be strangely different than those to whom they had been accustomed. Dark-skinned children and adults alike would hawk the wares of the islands in an effort to capture the interest of the affluent visitors from another land of which they knew nothing except by hearsay, where curio shops would abound, where the delightful breezes from the sea transfix those who are fortunate enough to avail themselves of the privilege.

After a fortnight, the vessel returned from whence it came and discharged its passengers once again into the work-a-day world where there were only memories. But what memories they were!

School days, graduations, vacations were now all events of the past, and William was now anxious to begin his new adventure. Carter too was anxious that William begin training in order that he might have ample time for adequate instruction and experience before Carter would find it necessary to relinquish the reins of the business to one whose life was yet ahead. The first day of William's experience as assistant and understudy to the older Mr. Wellington was marked by a festive air at the bank and included a welcoming party in the evening to introduce the new second-in-command to the clients and dignitaries of the city.

An appropriately prominent news item appeared on the front page of the *Wellington City Courier* on the day following:

> The citizens of Wellington City and the surrounding area are indeed proud to welcome William Carter Wellington, son of James Carter Wellington, as assistant to his father at the Wellington City National Bank. Young Wellington's acceptance of the position represents the seventh generation of the family to become identified with the institution which has meant so much to the growth and stability of our community. This area has been fortunate to have enjoyed these many years the progress afforded by the spirit of this pioneer family.

11.

As ANXIOUS AS HE WAS that his son succeed as his assistant and eventually as his successor as president of the bank, J. Carter Wellington was no more anxious than the young man himself. Even though both father and son worked hard to acquaint the latter with the day-to-day operations of the bank, it soon became evident that drastic action must be taken to accomplish their goals.

Not only was the older Wellington anxious that his son succeed, it was vitally important that he succeed if the family institution was not to fall into the hands of another dynasty. It was inevitable that the day was not far off when J. Carter would want, or even find it necessary, to lessen his responsibilities for a more relaxing life. His wife, Jane, was also anxious for her husband to exchange his duties at the bank for other interests which could be enjoyed by the two of them.

That drastic action must be taken if William was ever to fill his father's place was certain. What was not certain was what the drastic action would be. After much agonizing over the matter, Carter had an inspiration. He would assign that brilliant young lady whom he had hired recently to assist his son in his duties. "What was her name? Oh, yes, Susan Peters."

Susan had demonstrated unusual talent. Often it happens that in spite of adverse circumstances there are those who rise above them. Born in a coal-mining town of West Virginia, Susan was one of the younger children of a large family. The family, living on the edge of poverty, was particularly hard-hit by the continuing economic decline of the area following World War II, as were many families of that area. Along with hundreds of others, the family was forced to migrate to another area in search of a livelihood. The girl's parents packed their meager possessions and as many of the family members as possible in a battered and unreliable truck and proceeded in the direction of Pittsburgh. It was necessary for some of the older boys to remain behind for lack of space in the old conveyance. Later, they would hitchhike to join their parents. Since Pittsburgh offered little or no employment for this unskilled father, the family continued still northward, skirting the foothills of the Alleghenies, and arrived eventually in Wellington City, where the overloaded vehicle refused to travel farther.

Because Wellington City had also felt the effects of a declining population due to lack of work, a number of homes had been abandoned; one of these became the Peters' home simply because it was available, dilapidated as it was. Here in Wellington City the father managed to find a few odd jobs which, with some subsistence farming and some help from public sources, enabled him to support his family meagerly.

The younger members of the family, including Susan, were enrolled in the public school which they attended until such time as the law permitted their withdrawal. With one exception, education failed to interest the children, or for that matter, the parents. Susan was that exception. Despite the discouragement of her parents, who held that education beyond a basic need to learn the skills of reading and writing was unnecessary, especially for a girl, Susan remained in school. For practical reasons, she chose a secretarial and accounting course, so that she would be trained for office work, for Susan knew that her schooling beyond high school was out of the question. She was fortunate to be able even to complete high school.

Susan was an exceptional student. The classification "exceptional" includes a wide disparity of meaning, such as the student whose learning capacity leaves much to be desired. But Susan was not the latter type of student. Her learning capacity was the envy of her classmates. In fact, her teachers were amazed at the ease with which she was able to absorb her lessons, even to the point of putting the instructors to shame. For this reason, and because of her economic need, she was employed in the school office as a part of a youth program underwritten by the government.

Soon after Susan's graduation from high school, the

91

Wellington City National Bank was in need of some temporary help and solicited the graduating class of the local high school for some qualified young women. Susan's teachers spoke to the personnel office of her unusual ability, and the bank decided to give her an opportunity to prove herself; prove herself she did.

Susan was an unusual young lady in many ways. Besides being attractive and having outstanding academic ability, somehow she had acquired poise and social grace far beyond that which would be expected from one with such a background. All of these qualities earned her a niche in the hearts of those with whom she came in contact. It didn't take her many weeks to become a most valued employee, even superior, in many respects, to some of the seasoned personnel. But Susan remained modest at all times. During the time Carter's personal secretary was absent on vacation, he employed Susan as a substitute, a task which she performed notably. While explaining a complicated operation of the bank, Carter realized that here was a young lady that possessed the ability to grasp even the most difficult tasks. Following this demonstration of her unusual alertness, as well as her ability to work with others, Carter decided to retain Susan as a permanent employee.

"How remarkable," he mused, "that a person, in spite of the misfortune to be born and reared in the poorest of circumstances, has been able to overcome the handicap and has the promise of a useful, happy life, able to cope in any level of social or business environment." So impressed was he with the girl that he even mentioned her achievements to Jane.

Upon the return of Miss Jones, Carter's longtime secretary, Susan was assigned to other duties, assured of a place of responsibility at the bank. But she did not forget the needs of her family and those especially of her parents. She continued to aid them with financial support for those family members who were yet in the home. Susan found it quite difficult to maintain her personal appearance in keeping with expectations in the bank office, what with the numerous demands upon her salary. But Jane, who sensed Susan's feeling of inferiority because of her inability to dress as well as her co-workers, privately and tactfully assisted the girl, not only financially, but with small gifts of clothing at appropriate times, which Susan gratefully accepted.

Carter's idea was to place Susan and William in a secluded room in the rear of the bank. It would appear to other employees that the girl was William's secretary, but actually she would be doing any work that did not necessitate meeting the public. How could Carter lose? How could William be exposed to the many duplicate procedures day after day and not absorb at least a portion of the operational duties? As Carter's official assistant, William would have authority to sign documents, but Susan would process and prepare all the transactions, the usual duty of a secretary under any circumstance. The result would be that, to all appearances, the son of J. Carter Wellington would be falling right in step with his father. So the plan was put into practice and, indeed, seemed to be working quite well. Only three persons knew that appearances were deceiving—William, Susan, and J. Carter—and those three individuals were pledged to silence regarding the truth of the matter.

Susan experienced mixed emotions about the arrangement. It was not that she objected to carrying the responsibility while someone else reaped the financial benefits, but Susan had been taught to be honest and forthright; yet she desperately needed the employment and could ill afford not to acquiesce. Employment, especially for a young inexperienced girl, was hard to find in those times of economic stress in the area. At the same time her heart went out to the handsome young man who apparently was giving the challenge all he had, but yet found the work extremely difficult. Susan not only fulfilled her duties but also did her best to review each procedure time and time again to William, who after a time exhibited exceptional improvement.

Susan was proud of the progress William was making, limited though it was. The fact that William was some four years her senior was not important to either of them. After a time, the relationship between the two became more than a mere business association. As William learned to depend on Susan, he began to feel a deep affection for the young lady. Never before, as an adult, had he been showered with so much attention, or felt so close to anyone except, of course, his parents.

Two years passed during which William had fallen deeply in love with Susan. Susan felt the same toward William, but practicality dictated that the relationship could go no farther. In her opinion, the wide gap between the two, socially and economically, precluded a full-blown romance.

William may not have been a mental genius, but he had the capacity to love and to know that he needed Susan. At last he summoned the courage to reveal his feelings toward her.

"Susan, I have had something on my mind and in my heart now for many weeks. I don't know how to tell you except to say I love you! Each day my love for you grows deeper. What difference does it make that we were reared under different circumstances? What does make a difference is that I love you now. I love you so much I want to spend my life with you. In plain language, will you marry me?"

William's rather crude, unpoetic, and unromantic manner of proposing caught Susan unprepared. "Oh, William!" was all that she could manage to say at the moment.

Most young ladies would have been highly complimented by such an offer, and indeed Susan was. But there was the wide difference in their upbringing, as William had mentioned, indicating that he at least had thought about the difference. Still, William had been so much a part of her life during the past two years. Because of her mixed feelings of protection and love, she wanted to accept the offer, but her better judgment would not permit her to do so. She feared that the socially prominent James Carter Wellington family would feel that she had unduly influenced their son for financial advantage and would never accept her.

After a few moments Susan's voice returned. She reluctantly began, "William, your parents would feel I was taking advantage of you to better my economic position. I have much respect for your father and want to maintain that respect. While I don't know your mother as well, the contacts I have had with her have been very pleasant and she has been very thoughtful of me and my welfare. I want all that to remain the same."

William, tenderly embracing and kissing her, comforted her by saying, "Dear, it is our lives we must live and this very night I will tell them of my feelings for you."

"I would consent to our marriage only if your parents approve. Otherwise, I must sever my employment at the bank, as much as I need it, because the situation would be too difficult emotionally for us both."

"Dear," William responded, "either I succeed in winning my parents' approval or my banking career at the Wellington City National Bank is over. I will seek employment elsewhere. Perhaps that will help to persuade my parents to accept you."

But did either William or Susan really know, or realize, what they were saying?

Susan was firm in her stand: no parental approval, no marriage, and termination of her employment at the bank. At that, William, after kissing her, took his leave to go home to confront his parents with his desperate plight. Upon hearing William's story, in which he told of his great love for Susan and her rigid position regarding the approval of his parents, Carter retorted, "William, after all the support we have given you, with the right and proper training, and the economic and social position we enjoy, why would you consider such a poverty-stricken and social outcast for a life partner? It just wouldn't be a successful marriage. I realize you are an adult, and past the age where we can control your actions. We cannot dictate whom you marry, but you do not, and never will, have our approval or our blessing upon such a union, and you must face the consequences of your deeds."

But the word *never* is one of those famous last words.

"Okay, if that is the way you feel. But in my opinion, Susan is a fine, high-principled young lady, and I believe you, Father, will have to admit that. Money doesn't necessarily make one lovely, nor the lack of it unlovely. I am advising you now that I am departing from the bank and from this household this very night! Susan and I will solve our own problems. Good-bye!" he shouted as he started for the stairs to his room.

Carter and Jane could not believe their ears. It was apparent that their son was determined. "Wait, William! Let your mother and me discuss this matter alone for a while before making any decisions you might regret later."

"Okay, I'll give you five minutes. Meanwhile, I'll start packing! Let me know what you decide."

Carter and Jane heard his hurried steps as he proceeded to the top of the stairs, entered his bedroom, and slammed the door. They could also hear the sounds of dresser drawers opening and closing and doors slamming, along with heavy, hurried foot-steps.

It was not William who was about to make any regrettable decisions. Carter's first thought was to give an unequivocal disapproval of the match, or was it even a match? A match is the association of two similar objects. Carter was astounded that William was even capable of asserting himself in a manner he had never exhibited before. Where was the obedient, co-operative, child they had reared? Had he grown up as all children do? It was difficult for the parents to realize their son was no longer a child.

Now it was Jane's turn to speak. "Carter," she began, "you know Susan much better than I. What is your complaint against the object of our son's love, other than her lack of social and economic status? You yourself have related to me how well the two have gotten along. In spite of all the tutors, military schools, special college programs, libraries, to mention only a few programs in which William has participated, Susan has done for him what none of these was able to do. She has been able to stimulate him to a degree we never thought possible. It takes a strong character to let common sense rule the affections of the heart. I have the deepest respect for the girl in refusing to marry William without our goodwill, which would mean a lifetime of unhappiness for us all. Either we swallow our pride and bless the marriage to keep our son and gain a daughter, which we have never had, or we keep our pride and lose them both. Susan has been the means by which William, rather than being merely our son, has become a person in his own right. Anyhow, those who would ostracize us for admitting a girl of Susan's stature into our family are not worthy to be called our friends. Have you ever thought of the matter from that perspective?"

"Well, Jane, you do have a point. Suppose we arrange for William to bring Susan here for dinner tomorrow evening so the four of us can discuss the matter."

"Fine," replied Jane. "I can then become better acquainted with Susan."

With that Carter proceeded up the stairs and knocked lightly on the door of William's room. Carter related the substance of his and Jane's discussion. William took his father's hand and squeezed it warmly, elated that Susan had been invited to join them at dinner the next evening.

The dinner was served in an elegant manner Susan had never experienced. She was fearful the Wellingtons would notice that she was not acquainted with the social graces of dining as dictated by the books of etiquette, even though she had made an effort to become so during the last twenty-four hours, by a visit to the local library to consult a book on the subject. Nevertheless, if her lack of these amenities were noticed, it was overlooked. The Wellingtons were extremely cordial and Susan felt at ease by dessert time. The conversation consisted of small talk about subjects of general interest. The evening was a reminder of another evening some twenty-five or more years ago when another young lady had invited a young man to dine with her.

After dinner Susan felt strangely uncomfortable as the four of them retired to the living room. Would she be asked to relate details of her upbringing and her family life? But her concern was unfounded.

After a short period of silence when each cast glances at the other, Carter began the conversation. "So you two think you want to spend your lives together in the same house?"

"We most certainly do," replied William. "Susan is the girl I have been looking for. I really can't describe my feeling for her, but I know that no one has ever affected me as she has. You were in love too, once, were you not, Father? And I believe you are still in love with Mother. Can you describe the feeling?"

William's query really did not require a reply.

Then Jane asked Susan, "And do you feel the same about William, Susan?"

"Oh, of course, Mrs. Wellington. William is the only man I ever loved, or even had any serious interest in becoming associated with. But I will not marry him without the blessing of his parents."

"Well," responded Carter, "I did once fall in love and even though William's mother and I were more or less of the same background, I believe I would have still loved her had she not been. William is correct when he says that I am still in love with her. For that reason you and William can depend upon the blessing of both of us, and we will be honored to count you as our daughter. Right, Mother?"

Jane, her voice filled with deep emotion, stammered her reply in the affirmative.

Susan and William were deliriously happy as they left later in the evening to reveal the news to Susan's parents who, needless to say, were nonplussed that their daughter was to be so fortunate as to marry into a family such as the Wellingtons.

The situation was embarrassing. Carter and Jane would have been happy for Susan's parents to announce the impending marriage by means of a formal invitation to the wedding directed to members of the two families and their friends. But Susan's parents did not possess the means to give their daughter the kind of wedding the Wellingtons wished the couple to have. Neither had Susan been able to save enough from her modest salary to finance such an elaborate affair. While the Wellingtons would have been glad to arrange and finance the wedding, the propriety of doing so had to be considered. While Carter and Jane were mulling the perplexing problem in their minds, the doorbell in the front hallway rang. When Maria, the maid, answered the summons, she found a young man in green uniform who asked her to sign her name on a sheet, which he carried on a clipboard. She was then handed a yellow window envelope which she carried to Carter. Nervously he opened the envelope. He read it silently and then commented to Jane, "Well, our worries about a wedding are over." He then read aloud:

PITTSBURGH, PA.

MR. AND MRS. CARTER WELLINGTON. SUSAN AND I MARRIED THIS P.M. RETURN IN TWO WEEKS.

WILLIAM

The announcement of the marriage was duly reported according to the policy of small-town newspapers, whose reporters glean the information from the records of vital statistics in the area. Thus it didn't take long for all of Wellington City to become aware of the union. News readers could hardly believe their eyes. They asked one another, "Did you see . . . ?"

Especially astonished were Susan's schoolmates, who remembered her as a brilliant student and who coveted her ability to grasp ideas in spite of her disadvantaged home life. It was indeed a Cinderella story, one in which the heroine's coach had not turned into a pumpkin and the six white horses had not turned into six white mice at the stroke of midnight, with the beautiful maiden still wearing her glass slipper. Unlike the poor servant girl of the fairy tale, Susan was accepted by rich and poor alike, and especially by the Wellington family and, after the initial shock, its socially elite friends.

Even though Carter and Jane, along with their friends and relatives, were not privileged to be a part of an elaborate wedding party, their disappointments were forgotten when William and Susan were feted with a post-wedding reception upon their return from a glorious honeymoon, which took place not in London, not in Paris, but in a simple cabin in the Allegheny foothills.

12.

HONEYMOONS AND WEDDING parties must end and the participants must come down out of the clouds to face reality. It was no different with Susan and William Wellington. The couple set to the task of establishing a home in a new apartment in a building recently constructed as a part of Wellington City's expansion and renewal program, undertaken some years after the close of the great conflict known as World War II. They had rented the apartment even before their elopement, asking for the rental agency's promise of silence about the matter.

Susan especially was truly in ecstasy as the couple went about furnishing and decorating the spacious living quarters. She had never lived in such beauty and convenience. It was indeed a contrast to those homes to which she had been accustomed, which had usually been cramped, poorly furnished, run-down abodes in decaying neighborhoods.

But William's duties at the bank were beckoning. Both he and Susan had prepared for the day when William must handle his duties alone. Propriety dictated that a Wellington wife not be found in the marketplace for the purpose of earning a salary. It was arranged between the couple that William would bring home work he was unable to handle at the close of the business day and which Susan could supervise or even perform. Her husband would then carry back the completed task to the bank the following day. No one else, except William's father, realized that which was taking place.

Since Susan was not immediately available for consultation, William of necessity learned to handle many of the procedures himself. When he did not understand or was unsure of himself, he would delay his final decision with the excuse, "We'll have to have a little time on this;" or "We'll have to give this matter further consideration. I will call you when the document is ready." Invariably, the piece of business would be ready the following day after Susan had had an opportunity to peruse the matter and advise him.

Thus William did very well; he was a little slower, perhaps, than J. Carter, but his performance was of the same quality for which the Wellingtons had been known for generations.

Susan was a little reluctant for a time to join the social group of businessmen's wives, but little by little, at Jane's urging and encouragement, she learned to enjoy her new life. Mother and "daughter" were often seen together enjoying each other as well as the fellowship of other women with common interests.

J. Carter, Jane, William, and Susan were often a congenial foursome at various entertainment spots such as the theater, restaurants, dinner parties, sports events, and even played golf together when the weather permitted. Although this sort of life was new and strange to Susan, she enjoyed every minute of it. Nevertheless, she felt a little guilty that her parents and other members of her family were unable to enjoy this kind of life. But if luxury has never been available to one, it is often not missed, and there was no feeling of jealousy on the part of Susan's less fortunate family for she was not one to neglect or forget her obligations to them.

It was not long before the senior Wellingtons were informed they were to become grandparents. Indeed they were happy, but yet somewhat fearful. Would the child inherit William's handicap? Or would Susan's unusual capabilities be passed down to her child? Even if the child possessed only normal aptitudes, they would be satisfied, and they would be more than grateful if they were favored with something more. But the new grandparents-to-be would not let possibilities cancel their joy. They hoped, of course, that the first child would be a boy in order to carry on the family tradition, but they were not prepared for twin boys. In memory of their great-grandparents, the new members of the family were christened James Carter II and William Porter. Carter's and Jane's anxiety and, of course, that of the babies' parents, was relieved after the physician's examination revealed no apparent defects in either of the children. It was too soon to ascertain whether or not either child would be unusually brilliant, but the potential was at least present.

Like every grandmother, Jane was full of pride for her grandchildren, and as the years passed, each child achieved at least normal and, in many respects, above normal development.

Time was taking its toll for Carter and his productive years were nearing the end. The time for relinquishing the reins of the operation of the bank to another was slowly but surely approaching. William was appointed the new president and chairman of the board. Carter was somewhat apprehensive at William assuming the responsibility of president of the bank despite his faith in Susan's guidance from the sidelines. Susan, however, was of the opinion that the time had come to use her talents to the fullest in aiding her husband full-time at the bank. She also declared that she felt the time had come to recognize ability even though it was possessed by a woman. Jane, remembering her own similar situation upon graduating from college and being denied a position in the Porter Chair Company, overruled her husband's objections and supported Susan's decision fully. Finally, Carter, who realized the folly of resisting the entire family, including William himself, conceded and Susan became the second ranking officer at the bank.

To the surprise of nearly everyone, Susan had broken the tradition of her sex in assuming the position of Executive Vice President. The husband and wife team, unusual for the day, was a success and was accepted as an asset to the bank, and helped to give impetus to the cause of the rights of women to compete in the business world.

The Porter Chair Company had previously been merged with another firm and was no longer a responsibility of Carter and Jane. Their only responsibility now was to assist William and Susan in rearing the twins, a no small concern, but an enjoyable one. Welcome were the reports of the twins' outstanding progress in school, from the very first. Carter attributed their unusual abilities to the genes of their mother, but Jane reminded her husband that the Wellingtons and Porters had not been exactly failures.

At an advanced age, Carter became the victim of the same

fate that had removed his father from the scene, but he had taken much satisfaction in the knowledge that one day his grandchildren would be able to follow in his footsteps. With the rapid progress of the twins in their educational pursuits, all early fears had been dispelled and all evidence pointed to the fulfillment of the dream that at the Wellington National Bank, the family chain would remain unbroken.